# DANIEL

Legacy, Book 3

RJ SCOTT

Love Lane Books

# Copyright

## Dedication

*Always, for my family.*

# RJ SCOTT

## The Third Legacy
### DANIEL

Love Lane Books

## Chapter One

**Eight years ago**

*I WANT TO GO HOME.*

Daniel Chandler trudged miserably down the long black ribbon of road, tears burning his eyes, and hopelessness tightening his chest. The heat of an August Texas day had subsided to a slightly cooler evening, and the sky was a brilliant mass of stars, but he couldn't bring himself to look up at them anymore.

How had everything gone this badly wrong? Brett had promised that he would take Daniel somewhere far away from his foster family, but one weird question from an inquisitive cashier at a gas station and Brett had panicked. He'd refused to go any further, and said he was going home.

Daniel didn't want to go back to San Antonio. He wanted freedom, and the ability to decide for himself where his life was going. He'd overheard his foster parents talking about how he was a liability; that he costed them more than they made, and he knew it was only a matter of time before they got rid of him anyway.

So he refused to leave with Brett and got out of the car.

Brett didn't care, and he drove away, leaving Daniel stranded.

Daniel kicked a stone, stumbling a little when he misjudged the curve of the road. He'd eaten the cereal bars that Brett had tossed him and used up all the water. Which left him in the heat, without food or drink, and carrying a backpack with limited clothes. He also had books—his favorites, and a wallet which contained nothing more than a couple of hundred dollars he'd saved from his gardening job. The only official thing he had in the bag was his ID.

He'd left his most recent home at six-thirty a.m., with no real idea of where he was going or what he was doing, only knowing he wasn't going to spend another minute in a house where he wasn't wanted.

Hunching his shoulders against the weight of his backpack, he carried on. Sometimes he hummed to a song in his head. Other times he counted the steps he took, but most of the time he stared ahead, not counting or humming at all.

A car pulled up alongside him. No, a truck, and at first his heart leaped. Brett was back. He'd changed his mind and returned to help Daniel.

A female voice called out. "Can we give you a lift somewhere?" she asked through the open window.

Daniel saw she wasn't much older than he was, long blonde hair swept up into a ponytail, her smile wide, her expression kind. A man sat in the driver's seat, but he was in the shadows, and at first, Daniel couldn't make out his face until he leaned forward. The first thing Daniel noticed was the dog collar, then the same kindly smile as the girl. They were clearly related, both fair, with light eyes and an angular balance to their features.

"Hello, young man. My daughter and I are heading to Laredo. Would you like us to take you?"

He smiled at Daniel, this man in black with the white collar. This was an *average* family. They probably thought he was a hitchhiker and were offering genuine help. If Daniel couldn't trust a man of the cloth traveling with his daughter, then who could he trust? He scanned the road behind him, waiting for Brett to suddenly appear and pick him up, but he was tired, hungry, and verging on desperate.

"Thank you." Daniel opened the back door. He'd never hitchhiked before, didn't know what the etiquette was, but he felt like he should offer to pay. "I can cover gas," he said.

"No need for that," the dad said and extended a hand awkwardly over the seat, which Daniel shook. "Father Frank Martins and this is my daughter Andrea."

Andrea glanced back at him and grinned again. "Hey."

"Daniel," Daniel replied, as mute as usual around a girl as he was with boys. She turned back to the front, and Frank put the truck in drive.

"Buckle up," he said.

Daniel did as he was told. Then settled back for the ride.

"Where are you from?" Frank asked after a few moments of silence, filled only with the soft sound of tires on blacktop.

"San Antonio," Daniel answered.

"Really? What brings you this far south?"

Andrea shushed her dad, "Stop asking him questions, Daddy."

Her dad huffed a gentle laugh. "Sorry." He used the mirror to see Daniel. "You like music?"

Daniel nodded, thankful to Andrea for running interference.

Frank fiddled with the stereo. Country music filled the cab, and Frank hummed along. Andrea was on her phone, as evidenced by the glow of light as screens changed, and Daniel regretted leaving his phone at home. In his mad, *stupid*, anger, he'd wanted no way for his foster parents to keep tabs on him, but right now, he kind of wished he could phone them. He should pluck up the courage and ask Andrea to borrow hers. Maybe give his foster-parents a quick call, apologize, get them to pick him up, or at least arrange a bus.

They would help him. He didn't doubt that. Even if he'd been an idiot and they wanted to hand him off to the next family, they would never leave a fourteen year old kid stranded miles from home.

"You thirsty?" Frank asked, and before Daniel could answer, Frank had unlocked the glove box and pulled out a bottle of water, passing it back to Daniel.

He took it with grateful thanks and downed a third of it in thirsty gulps. They reached the outskirts of a small town, and the car slowed to a stop outside a cookie-cutter house, a pretty place with manicured lawns.

Andrea turned around to look at Daniel.

"This is where I get out," she announced. "Nice to meet you, Daniel."

*I thought they were both going on to Laredo?*

Frank turned around as well. "I can take you all the way into the city. It's only another ten minutes or so to the bus station or somewhere like that? A hostel?"

"I'm not sure—"

Frank interrupted, "Or you could stay the night here or a motel. We have one a few blocks down from here."

Andrea shut the door and jogged up to the house, vanishing inside.

"Could I just borrow your phone?" Daniel asked.

Frank smiled, nodded, and pulled out his phone, tutting as he did so. "Oh my, the phone's dead. You want to use my house phone? Or shall I just get you to the city? The bus station, right? They have public phones there."

So many decisions. So many difficult choices, he thought and yawned.

"Yeah." Daniel just wanted to get home.

"Yeah, what?" Frank prompted.

Daniel blinked at him. He was tired, and everything felt kind of hazy. "Yeah, home." Back to his pretend parents and his pretend family, but back to a warm bed.

"Come on. Get in the front here."

Daniel did as he was told, his limbs feeling heavy, and his coordination shit. Finally, he was belted in the front, and he closed his eyes briefly, exhaustion washing over him.

"That's a good boy," Frank murmured. "You sleep now."

The country music got quieter, Frank's humming was louder, and the journey to the city took a long time, the car swaying, and Daniel's head thicker, full of softness and a weird kind of peace. He saw fields and signs, but none of them made any sense. Finally, he couldn't fight the overwhelming lethargy, so he slept.

And woke up in hell.

## Chapter Two

**NOW**

COREY DRYDEN LEANED INTO HIS SISTER, TAKING A moment of comfort from Amy for himself. Everyone expected him to be the strong one today, but she'd seen through his forced bravery. She probably knew that what he really wanted to do was find a corner, curl into a ball, and cry.

The funeral was done, and the well-wishers, some he didn't know, had left. The big house was empty, caterers told to go, everything as spotless as when their mom had been in charge.

It was just them. Him, and his three sisters.

Abruptly, he was the head of this family at the age of twenty-five, and he'd faked it today, right up until an hour ago.

*"This is all yours now,"* Austin said as if that was a good thing. The family lawyer was trying to help, but when Corey didn't reply, he at least had the grace to be

ashamed and apologized, but of course, Corey had excused the words.

People were grieving, and he had to be the strong one and allow everyone else to have their time to mourn. *"Your father and uncle knew they were leaving Dryden-Marsdale in good hands."* Austin reminded him.

In good hands? Corey wasn't long out of college, interning temporarily at a tech company, looking for what to do with his life. In his heart he wanted to write, was desperate to create stories that maybe he could one day sell. He didn't see Dryden-Marsdale, a firm specializing in asset management, as the rest of his life.

Not that he had any choice now.

"Are you going to be okay?" Amy asked, her soft voice enough to pull him out of his thoughts. He realized he was staring at the office door, their dad's sanctum, where deals were made and paperwork sat in piles on his desk. He'd never been the tidiest of men, but then he'd also never shut the door on his wife and kids. Many a day, Corey and the girls would sit in the office with him, reading books, or on their laptops doing homework. So much so that their dad had set aside a part of the room just for them, with desks and chairs.

When Corey was little, he and his dad had built a blanket fort in there, and they'd even allowed girls in, much to his mom's amusement. Of course, Chloe, the youngest sister at that time , filled her diaper, threw up her milk, and the blanket fort was done for the day. Still, the memory was a good one, his dad in there with him talking about cars and sports and life in general.

"I'll be fine," Corey lied.

"I can help," Amy murmured.

Corey wanted to do this alone, not in a selfish way. The four Dryden siblings, him, Amy, Chloe, and Sophie, all deserved to be in the office together. He was just doing what was expected of him, protecting his sisters from things they shouldn't have to deal with.

"I've got this," he murmured and pulled her into a hug.

"You don't need to do this alone, Corey."

The sound of footsteps on the wooden floor had them both turning. Sophie only six, and the baby of the family, was in oversize slippers, her pajamas, Oscar-Teddy in her hand, and her face pale. "I can't sleep," she said, and tears collected in her eyes, rolling down her face.

Corey and Amy exchanged glances, and Amy nodded imperceptibly, *I got this.* She scooped up their sister and walked down the hall, promising a story and chocolate. When their voices had faded, Corey turned the handle, and eyes shut, he stepped inside and closed the door behind him.

When he opened them again, he didn't know what he'd thought he'd see. Nothing had changed. There was no sign of anything to indicate his parents and uncle were dead. No significant shift in the air, or whispers of ghosts.

It was only an office.

Floor-to-ceiling bookcases on one side, full of bright novels, selected kids' books, and black folders for his dad's work, a filing system Edward Dryden had never quite gotten a handle on, much to his wife's consternation. Emily Dryden was the organized one in the house. She had to be, with a husband who was away a lot, four children, and her numerous charitable associations. She never worked for Dryden-Marsdale, even though she'd been a Marsdale before marrying Edward. Their joined initials could be seen everywhere in this room; the double E's looped around each other and intertwined. The design mirrored how they'd been in life.

To the left of the office was the area Dad had put aside for the kids. He'd thrived on the chaos of having people in the room with him; conference calls with Sophie hanging off his neck had been a frequent occurrence. He wasn't sure Uncle Drake had been as impressed with how his brother worked, but he'd never married or had kids, as far as anyone knew. Tightly restrained, Uncle Drake was the one who found organization in the chaos and had become Edward's, right-hand man.

The windows looked out to the manicured lawns beyond and the summer house by the large pond at the bottom of the garden. Emily Dryden had loved her oasis of peace. Tiny fairy lights following a path from the house to the pond had been strung individually by her. They weren't on now, leaving the yard in darkness and the office gloomy apart from the soft light from a full moon. He couldn't see her roses from there, tucked away behind a neatly trimmed hedge in the sunniest part of the garden. The area wasn't meant to be viewed from the house; it was the place she went to read, and what had become her own private space.

*Someone needs to check on the roses.*

He flicked on the desk light and slid into his dad's chair.

*My chair. It's my chair.*

He didn't know where to start with the desk, or the company, or life. He only knew he had to start somewhere.

*Anywhere.*

Pulling a piece of paper toward him, he waited, pen poised, for inspiration. He should make a list of company issues. The fact that Dryden-Marsdale had a whole raft of ongoing contracts was a priority. The company was strong, but how did it come back from losing its founders and principal shareholders? The man who had guided the company to what it was now, his wife, and the operating manager.

Grief hollowed Corey, and the pen in his hand wobbled. Where did he start? With the company? The house? The rose garden? The trusts for his two youngest sisters? Did he get someone in here to help him wade through the mess of it all? Or did he leave his job and make this his complete focus? How could he do that when he had to hold Sophie as she cried, or entice his sisters to eat when he didn't even want to feed himself?

Then he realized there was something more important than the company. A part of him that had to be the priority. He wrote his first heading.

*Family.*

Somehow, the four of them made it through week one. Corey had arranged counseling for his sisters and knew that at some point he would need to talk to someone as well. One day when he didn't have the weight of the company on his shoulders.

He hadn't been into the central offices of Dryden-Marsdale, on the twenty-ninth floor of a glass-and-steel tower in the center of Dallas. His dad's PA, Heather, was watching over things and coordinating the team leaders of the fifty or so staff members who were shaken but pulling together. Heather said he didn't need to worry just yet. That he needed to give himself time.

She prepared reports for him, told him what stage contracts were at, and by the time he'd passed the first week, he'd begun to turn a corner. He'd even made some limited sense of his dad's filing, which was a lot more organized than it had appeared. The black box from the plane was found, on day fifteen after the funeral, damaged and embedded into the soft dirt on top of bedrock, but they hadn't heard anything yet on what was in it or why their parents' plane had ended up crashing. The prevailing hypothesis was engine failure, but no one actually *knew*.

He spun the chair to stare out over the garden, watching birds on the ornate feeder, seeing them bickering over a lack of food, and turning back, he added an item to his list. *Bird feed.* It wasn't the most important, but it wasn't as stupid as the item that read, *get a haircut*. He could live with longer hair, but the birds relied on his mom. Depended on the family.

*Everyone relies on the family.*

He stiffened at the knock on the door; the lawyer was there, and this was a *meeting*. The agenda was the will, the trusts that had been set up for the four children, and details of personal items that their parents had thought they might want one day.

A day in a far future. Not now. Not when their youngest child was only six.

Amy poked her head around the corner, and the tension in him slid away. Not the lawyer then.

"Chloe won't come out of her room."

The middle of his three sisters, Chloe had been quiet since the funeral, taking to sitting in her room and listening to rock music that at least filled the house with noise.

Without that, it would have been more mausoleum than home.

"I tried." Amy sounded sad. "I spoke to her for a long time about the future and how things were going to be okay." She crossed her arms over her chest, pale and looking way more fragile than he'd ever seen her.

He wanted to tell her to deal with Chloe because his head was pounding, and he wasn't sure he could handle Chloe right now. She'd gone from quiet to angry, and he had no idea how to break through to her. Nor would she speak to anyone, not a counselor, not even her family. But he couldn't say that to Amy. She'd done her best, and he squared his shoulders.

"It's okay. I'll talk to her."

He took the stairs slowly as if that would give Chloe time to come out of her room all on her own, but her door remained frustratingly closed.

He knocked.

"Go 'way, Amy," Chloe shouted.

Corey sighed. "It's me."

"Go away, Corey! Leave me alone."

"I'm giving you thirty seconds, and then I'm coming in."

"Please just go," she said again.

"Twenty."

He heard some noises, scrambling, and then he tried the handle. At least Chloe hadn't locked the door. When he opened the door, she was sitting on her bed, dressed in her familiar black, her legs crossed, and her hands on her knees. She looked composed, but mascara smeared her cheeks, and her eyes were red and puffy.

"Don't you *dare* ask me if I'm okay," she snapped.

That was the last thing he was going to ask her. They were all far from *okay*.

"We just need to get this done," he murmured as he sat on the bed next to her.

She reached for his hand, and he laced his fingers with hers. "I don't want to know what important thing they wanted me to have." She sniffed.

He handed her a tissue, then sighed heavily. "I don't either."

"I don't want *things*. I want *them*."

He squeezed her hand. What did he say? That listening to the bequests wasn't the end of a connection to their parents? How could he say that when he was just as scared to know what his parents' thoughts had been for their children?

"Let's do this together," he said, knowing what he was doing was wrong. He was encouraging her to push her grief away. To carry on. He should've been hugging her and talking through her fears, and his own.

But he couldn't do it.

She nodded, unlaced her fingers from his, and blew her nose. "Give me five," she said, and he saw that same steel in her that he had in himself. She would deal with today for now and leave tomorrow for when it came.

He pressed a kiss to her hair. "Love you, sis."

"Love you too," she mumbled, and they awkwardly side-hugged.

When he got back downstairs, the lawyer was there. Austin looked stoic but pale, his briefcase held in front of his body like a shield.

"Corey, how are you?"

Corey blinked at him, seeing in the other man what

was inside him, tightly coiled pain and grief. Austin had been a close friend of both Edward and Emily Dryden, had spent time in the house as a friend with his wife Mary, and their two children, both under ten. Corey imagined Austin went home each night and hugged his family close.

"We're managing," Corey lied. He felt like a big kid playing dress up and expected Austin to ruffle his hair or something.

Instead, Austin extended his hand and shook Corey's firmly. "Let's get this done, eh?"

Pleasantries over, they went into the office, where Amy was sitting with Sophie on her lap. Chloe followed them in, and finally, the four of them were there, with the beautiful gardens beyond.

The will basics were standard as expected. The estate, the company, everything was split equally, with Sophie and Chloe's in trust until they turned twenty-one. Then Austin cleared his throat and talked them through the items they'd explicitly been left. Amy, a necklace that had belonged to their great-grandmother, Chloe, their mom's ring. Sophie was left a bracelet that had been a wedding gift from their dad to their mom, and each of the girls had a personal letter as well. They didn't open the letters though, they quietly sat, even little Sophie, and stared at Corey.

Then it was Corey's turn. The memento was from his father, a key that would open the deep drawer next to his dad's side of the bed. His dad had written in journals each day, sometimes nothing more than a note of the weather, but often short stories about his children, what they'd done, what he'd seen. Corey knew they were in that drawer, and he'd share it all with his sisters. He pocketed the key and the letter his parents had written to him, resolving to read it when he had a quiet place.

Then, with Austin leaving, it was done.

Now they needed to get on with life.

---

Six weeks passed before Corey was in any kind of place to examine what his father had left him. He'd been seeing a counselor for two of those weeks and had spent a lot of his time in the office tower downtown. He hated sitting at the desk pretending to be in charge, but grief didn't allow him to think about an alternative. Somehow, he was muddling through the days.

The girls were all in bed, and he couldn't sleep, walking the corridors of the big house, stumbling a little with the exhaustion of pushing through, and it was only on his second pass by his parents' room that he stopped and peered inside.

It was just as it had been the day they'd left for Denver. The bed was made, but his mom's ordinarily immaculate dressing table still held the evidence of her packing. A drawer was slightly open, and he shut it, recalling the last morning, the kiss goodbye from her, the admonishment from his dad that he really needed to get a move on thinking about what he was going to do with his degree in English Literature.

Grief swallowed him whole, and the despair that came with it was too much for him to keep inside. He slid from the stool and curled up by the bed, rocking with the tears and thinking about that last time he'd seen his mom and dad.

How long he sat there he didn't know, but finally there were no more tears left. Numb, he levered himself up to sit on the side of the bed.

*What now?*

The key burned a hole in his pocket where he'd kept it since he'd been given it. Instinctively he knew that it was time to use it.

He unlocked the drawer, smiling a little at the haphazard pile of journals, taking out the top one and realizing it was the latest. The last words written were sharp and defined, a simple, *flying to Denver in the a.m. Sophie lost another tooth, and the tooth fairy visited.*

Normal life. Nothing that told a story of the man dying the next day. He flicked through the pages and set it to one side, pulling out the next, and another, lining them up in chronological order as best he could. He realized there was a journal missing, four years ago, September to March, but it was probably in the office somewhere. He'd need to find it for completion, and then maybe he and the girls could read them all together and laugh at the memories.

There was a letter addressed to both his parents from the University of Denver, thanking his dad for supporting something called the EE scholarship. This was the first Corey had seen that his parents' philanthropic works extended to a college that wasn't in the state they lived in.

He put the note to one side for safekeeping, determined the estate would keep the charity work up, as well as any other education program created and funded by his family. Also, he made a note on his phone to find out more about this. Who dealt with it? Was it Austin or another lawyer? Maybe it was a company thing?

He found one last envelope beneath the journals. Dull

gray, with no address on the front, and heavy with whatever was in it. On the reverse, a logo representing the Hart Detective Agency, Dallas. Why did his dad have an envelope from a PI? Intrigued, Corey tipped the contents onto the bed. The latest letter was dated only the week before his parents' death. A simple handwritten note, signed by a man called John McMillan, and the sentence, *as discussed re DDL.* DDL? Was that Drake Dryden? Uncle Drake? That was the only DD he knew, but what the L stood for he had no idea.

*Asshole.* The thought was uncharitable, given that his uncle had died in the same plane crash as his parents, but there was no getting away from it. Corey hadn't liked him much. A chronic gambler, Drake was a man who'd needed his brother to dig him out of more than a few holes.

Intrigued, Corey skimmed the contents of the envelope, details of past events, a list of scholarships stretching back a few years followed by question marks, and then words which grew progressively darker.

There were the photos in a separate wallet, and he pulled the first out and couldn't quite make out the blurry image there. He flicked on the bedside light for extra illumination, and his breath stuttered.

He fanned out the photos, young boys, with names and dates on the reverse, and only when he had every single one laid out on the bed, along with hospital reports and psychological assessments, did he begin to cry again.

But this time it wasn't grief. It was horror.

---

Riley Campbell-Hayes was a tall man who cut an

imposing figure in a tailored suit. He extended a hand immediately when Corey walked out of the elevator on the floor that housed CH Consulting. The company was something to do with oil and ethical exploration, and he knew who Riley was from the papers and the news. He'd been kidnapped in Mexico if Corey recalled rightly, and he was married to a man, and they had children. All that information was available online, and Corey had done his due diligence on the man he was coming to for help.

They shook hands, and Riley's hazel eyes were filled with the compassionate expression Corey was beginning to recognize in every person he met.

"I'm sorry for your loss," Riley said. "I met your father a few times in the course of investment and charity work. He was a good man."

Everything was too raw in Corey's head to answer. A good man wouldn't have hidden what his brother had done.

"Thank you."

"Coffee?" Riley asked as they walked past a bank of desks to an office at the back.

"No, thank you."

The office had glass walls, but the blinds were drawn, giving them privacy. Another man was in there already, one who Corey recognized immediately. John McMillan, the PI his dad had hired.

They'd had more than one meeting since Corey found the paperwork. Uncle Drake Dryden's life had unpeeled slowly and painfully in front of him.

On the surface, Drake had been a model businessman, a family guy, despite not having kids himself or a partner.

News articles highlighted that he did a lot for charity and loved his nieces and nephew.

No one had exposed the sordid side of Drake Dryden, and the whole mess was now his to unravel. Which was when the PI suggested they bring this to an interested third party who'd done their own kind of investigations.

Riley Campbell-Hayes and his husband, Jack.

Why the PI called for a meeting, why Riley Campbell-Hayes involved, Corey didn't know, but he was willing to follow all leads to get a full story in his head.

*Before I decide what to do next.*

Corey and John took seats, and a late arrival dashed in, a Stetson in hand and dust on worn jeans and dark hair.

"Apologies." The man extended his hand to John and then Corey. "Jack Campbell-Hayes," he said when no one introduced him.

Riley shut the door and sat down with Jack.

"What is this about?" Corey asked, feeling young, stupid, and out of place.

John cleared his throat, and then he spoke directly to Riley and Jack.

"I think I found something else connected to the Castille case."

Jack sat back in his chair as if his strings had been cut, and Riley exhaled noisily.

"Shit," Jack muttered with feeling.

"Who?" Jack asked, and his gaze shot to Corey.

"The scholarship details for the last year of Daniel's funding, and I'm sure I've found one of the abusers who visited the ranch in Laredo and hurt the boys."

Corey felt the tension grow, no one knowing what to say, Jack still staring at him.

Finally, Corey had enough of the heavy silence. "Will someone please tell me something? Anything?"

John sat forward in his chair and coughed again, his eyes bright with emotion. Then he addressed Corey directly.

"I'm sorry," he said.

And once more, as he listened, Corey's life began to crumble around him.

## Chapter Three

DANIEL LOVED THIS TIME OF THE MORNING. HE WAS always awake long before anyone else, and he'd make coffee in his tiny dorm room and carry it down to the square, rain or shine, to sit and contemplate life. The peace was perfect for Daniel to find his center, breathing in a slow rhythm and listening to the sounds around him.

There could be people coming back to their dorms late, some of the more sports-orientated students might get up early to make it to gyms or practices. But mostly, it was him and his coffee. The bench he liked to sit on was under an ancient oak, the kind found all over Denver U campus. In the summer, the leaves provided shade. In the winter it meant the bench was in parts devoid of snow under the thicker branches.

More often than not, he didn't *choose* to sit there. It wasn't a *choice* for him to go outside. Sometimes he had to get away from the curling posters on the wall, the lumpy single bed, or the row of Coke cans on his windowsill. Sometimes it was a desperation to find air, to be able to breathe, and on those mornings he would come down not even waiting to get coffee.

This morning was different. The dreams hadn't tipped over into nightmares. He hadn't woken drenched in sweat or crying. He even took the time to make a coffee with the small Keurig machine he'd bought out of his meager savings, earned from a summer job in the campus bookshop. It was good coffee.

In fact, this morning he felt strong. As if he could take on the entire world. He knew better than to assume this would last. All the counseling in the world couldn't stop the subconscious part of his mind from reminding him of his past every so often. A history that meant he had a private room, his own tiny cubicle of a bathroom, and was allowed dispensation in exams if he needed. He hadn't used that so far, but he was certainly happy to have his own room and shower.

Imagine waking up in the middle of a nightmare and some dude in another bed asking him what was wrong?

The latest round of dreams featured the guy he'd hooked up with on the weekend after he'd drunk enough not to care about pain or panic. This had been, by necessity, an off-campus, nameless fuck that had done nothing to release the tension building inside him this close to finishing college and being free to go off into the wide world.

At least dreaming of the short redhead was better than the nightmares.

"Hey."

Daniel scooted up the bench a little, allowing Georgina Everett room to sit, so there was plenty of space between them. She was a fellow runner, but where he was a long-distance runner, she was a sprinter. If anyone at the college could have been called a friend, it would've been her. She was sunshine and positivity to his caution, and she often joined him for five minutes on his bench. At first, it had angered him that she wanted to invade his privacy, but she didn't see his anger, and after a few months, it didn't matter anymore.

"Morning, G." She wasn't Georgina or George; she'd always been just G to him.

"I got you notes from a study group," she announced. She'd gotten used to his ways, knew there was no point in asking him to any study sessions or giving him time to find a reason not to go. She was a firm believer that human interaction was a good thing, and at first, she'd been utterly determined that she was going to drag him along with her. She'd given up now and gave him the notes, and she never asked him why he didn't want to meet up with other students in social groups.

He knew he was strange and absolutely understood that others found him weird. It genuinely didn't bother him. If people thought he was approachable they would be up in his personal space, wanting things from him, convinced he could be rational and sociable if only he tried.

*Who says I don't try? I try every day.*

"What's it for this time?" He asked.

"Ably's essay on Roman Britain." She rhythmically kicked the bench as she talked.

Professor Absalom was a complete bastard when it came to setting essays. His titles were all deceptively simple, but then they would come back marked as not covering X, or Y, or possibly Z. A study group meant they could cover all eventualities.

He'd already written his essay; all four thousand words had been done exactly one week after it had been set. That was his routine, and it kept him sane for the most part. She didn't have to know that, though.

"Thank you," he murmured.

"I'll email it to you." She couldn't understand why he didn't have a phone, but she'd stopped commenting on that after he'd said he was allergic.

People got away with being allergic to all kinds of things. Why not phones? She patted his leg and then was gone as though she'd never even existed and was merely a figment of his tortured imagination.

Not even *his* fucked-up imagination would be shitty enough to conjure up a bossy short girl who liked to pat his leg as if it didn't freak him out each time.

He finished his coffee, threw the dregs onto the grass, and sauntered back to his room. After all, he really did have all the time in the world. Today was lecture-free, a day to study, learn, and have peace and silence in the library. His perfect kind of day. He had a one-hour block in his planner to study Roman Britain, two hours on Iron Age Germany, thirty minutes for lunch, two hours free reading, and two hours on his career search. Every day was planned to the last minute, but at this moment, he had that delicious hour where he showered and read whatever the hell he wanted.

Right now, he was on a science fiction journey and had very nearly finished Philip K. Dick's entire backlist.

First though he'd tidy his room a little. Space was at a premium in the individual dorm rooms, and the furniture was economical in size, the bed short for his six-foot frame, the bathroom so small he had to shuffle in sideways. It helped to be organized, and apart from the Coke cans ready to be recycled, his room was immaculate. The posters he had inherited. Some band he'd never heard of and a full-length photo of a blonde woman, who according to Dave, the guy he'd gotten the room from, was one hot babe.

If he considered her dispassionately, then her face was undoubtedly equal left and right, and her hair flicked perfectly in all directions. He didn't want or need to brighten up his room. It was just a place where he slept.

There was a bed, a desk, and a nightstand with an alarm clock and a lamp. The clock he never had to use because his internal body clock was scarily accurate, and the light stayed on all night.

His sports equipment, really nothing other than three pairs of running shoes and immaculately folded gear, sat on the bottom shelf of his closet; the rest of his clothes in neat piles on the other shelves. Friday was wash day, but even his dirty laundry was folded, so it didn't take up too much room.

He had student-living down to a T.

The only real sign that a student lived there was the cork-board by the door which was ruthlessly separated into class schedules. It didn't have the usual collection of takeout menus, or party invites pinned to it. Daniel ate all his meals in the cafeteria and took away fruit and yogurts for his lunch. And he didn't do parties. Ever. Nope, his board had essay titles and a book list he marked when he'd finished a book. He wasn't the quickest or brightest student, but he worked damned hard to make sure he didn't betray the faith that had been given to him by the company that had offered him a scholarship for his first three years, and the next one who'd been over generous this last year.

Particularly as he'd gotten the money from each source with no strings attached, no promise to work for them, which was good, considering they were some kind of off shore investment company that were probably looking at the funding of an under privileged kid as a tax deduction.

He had no doubt they'd found out about his past somehow, not the gory details, but the whole foster care or group home situation. The money arrived regularly, and Daniel asked no questions. It might be charity, but he'd worry about it when he had a proper job and could pay it back.

His shower was hot for long enough to wash thoroughly, and wrapped in a towel, he sat on his desk chair and mentally ticked off the things he'd already done today. Coffee, sit on the bench, fake talking with G, shower.

Someone knocked on a door somewhere down the corridor, the sound of banging in the next room and arguments as the dorm woke up. He lived with a lot of freshmen, as most students in their last year had moved off campus in cliquey groups of five or so. No way was he going anywhere.

The knocking grew closer as if whoever was doing it was banging on each door searching for someone. Probably a drunk kid looking for his own damn room.

Then the noise was at his door, but it wasn't random banging. This was a precise double rap. If he sat there long enough, they would move on, but they seemed to be staying, and then to make matters worse, he heard Russell's voice.

"Yeah, I know he's in there. Saw him go in just now." Russell, the idiot guy from three doors down, knocked hard as if he was beating a drum. "Someone to see you, Danny-boy," he added loudly.

"Maybe he isn't in there," a second voice, soft but firm, said.

"Danny!" Russell knocked again. "He's fucking weird," Russell said, a little lower as if maybe Daniel wouldn't hear that.

Another bang, more shouting and eventually the whole freaking place would wake up and be milling around wanting to know what was up. Daniel knew he wasn't going to get away with sitting there. Pulling on some jeans and a T-shirt, he then crossed to the door and pulled the chair wedged under the handle out of the way. Then he flung it open before he could even think of second-guessing himself, and a nervy Russell jumped back a foot.

"Jesus dude, warn a guy," Russell gasped, but Daniel gave him a look that seemed to work most of the time. The one that said, back-off-I'm-creepy-strange-and-I-will-eat-you-alive.

Russell reacted as expected, slinking back and away to his own room. A couple of other doors were open, bleary-eyed students with interesting bed hair staring at the ruckus in the corridor. He stared them down as well, and they all closed their doors immediately.

"Are you Daniel?" the visitor asked. He was shorter than Daniel by at least three or four inches, his eyes green, his hair a messy head of near-black layers that curved around his face. He had money. Daniel could tell that from the high-end designer shirt and the pressed jeans, along with immaculate boots.

Yep. Money. Entitled, pushy, rich boy, at his door.

But also gorgeous, in that preppy way, and certainly the kind of man that Daniel would've been aiming to hook up with if it was the weekend, and if he wasn't at college, and if he didn't suffer panic attacks the minute the sex was over.

Sex was a means to an end, with guys who knew the score, random hookups, nothing serious. Hell, at least he could still have sex after what he'd been through. That was a positive.

*If only you didn't run after every hookup and actually stayed and maybe had a conversation.*

"There are a lot of Daniels on campus," Daniel murmured. "I don't know you, so I assume you have the wrong one."

"I was looking for Daniel Brown." He waited.

"Sorry, you have the wrong room," Daniel lied.

The visitor stepped forward a little. His foot was right where it would block the door from shutting, but there didn't seem to be antagonism in his eyes. If anything, he was distressed. He looked to be a little older than Daniel's twenty-two, but there were lines of exhaustion on his face, and he seemed fearful. A niggle of dread poked at Daniel's subconscious. The only time he'd seen fear like this had been in a courthouse years ago when he stood with three boys to give evidence against men who'd hurt them.

"Please, I want to talk. That's all."

Daniel pushed the door against his foot. He could take the guy down. He'd had training in self-defense. He wasn't some stupid, naive kid anymore.

"I think you need to leave," Daniel insisted and put more of his body weight against the wood.

The visitor held up a hand in defeat and then held out a card.

"My name is Corey Dryden. This is my card."

Daniel took the card because that could possibly expedite this stranger, Corey, leaving. But no, the guy was talking. He glanced past him to the hall. Everyone; everyone had disappeared from view, likely all back in bed, given it was still not much past six a.m.

"My parents died recently." He cleared his throat. "I don't know if you knew them. Edward and Emily Dryden?"

"Nope," Daniel said with conviction.

Corey's face fell. "Okay, I get that. I mean just because it was the center of my world, it doesn't mean... I found some... look..." Corey pushed a hand through his hair and judging from the messy flick to it, this was clearly something he did a lot. "I don't want to talk here. There's a coffee shop at the hotel just at the end of the block, outside the college. Hills Beans at the Morton Hotel. You know it?"

Daniel blinked at him. Everyone knew Hills Beans. It was expensive and didn't precisely cater to strapped-for-cash college kids like himself. Specifically more for the faculty and visiting speakers, along with the wealthier student who could afford five dollars for a coffee. The hotel was used by parents when their kids attended for orientation.

Corey waited a short moment and then sighed. "Will you please look up my parents online, me, my family, so you know who I am? I'd love to talk to you. I'll stay in Hills Beans all day. You can find me there, okay?"

"Go away." Daniel was clear and concise. That tone usually worked, but Corey didn't immediately move.

Instead, he scanned the hallway and then lowered his voice. "I know your real name is Daniel Chandler, okay? This is about what happened. Before."

Daniel's heart stopped, and he stared at Corey, checking for the lie in his eyes or the hell of the truth that he might know, and the panic started. Corey moved his foot out of the way, and Daniel slammed the door, locking it, shoving the chair back under the handle, and then falling right where he stood, curling into a ball and trying to breathe.

The walls closed in on him, and he scrambled to sit with his back to the closet and his eyes firmly on the window. No one could come in through the door, and he was two floors up; he was safe.

*I'm safe. I'm safe. They're dead or in prison. No one knows I'm here.*

His breathing restarted as reality made more sense, and the panic drifted away, all jagged edges, piece by piece. First, he settled his breathing. Next, he counted back from one hundred. Lastly, he uncurled himself and stretched his muscles.

*You knew one day you'd have to face the reality of the memories again.*

*You knew this.*

So much work on his fragile psyche, and he was still a panicking mess at the mention of his real name. Daniel Chandler was dead. He'd died the minute he stepped into Frank's car and looked into the soft eyes of his daughter. He'd died the minute he'd trusted.

He crawled to the bed and then checked the window,

unlocking it to open it a little and then locking it in the open position. He just needed to get some air, and a cool breeze drifted through the opening.

Black dots swam in his eyes, and he closed them, scrubbing at them and making it worse, then sat on his bed when his legs wouldn't hold him up any longer. He needed to call someone. Anyone. People from the courtroom where he'd given evidence, the ones who said they'd help him? Darren Castille? Or Jack Campbell-Hayes? But he'd run from them, made his own way, and he might have their numbers but he didn't need them or anyone else.

*I don't need them now. I don't need anyone.*

He stiffened his spine, then pulled his laptop toward him and turned the card until he found the name, Corey Dryden, and the whole mess was listed in a hundred results.

'Texas family tragedy after unexplained plane crash.'

The latest story was a news release. The pilot-owner, Edward Dryden, rumored to have deliberately flown a privately-owned jet plane into a mountain. Dying instantly, along with his wife, Emily, and his brother, Drake. Daniel didn't recognize the family, but he did recall seeing the news detailing the accident when it had first happened. He wasn't *that* buried in his education. It wasn't something that touched him, and he couldn't join the hysteria of finger-pointing that had taken over the press for a day or two.

Shaking his head, he focused back on the article.

The saddest part was the four children left behind. Corey, a son, twenty-five, then three daughters, Amy, Chloe, Sophie. Sophie was only six. There were photos of them at the funeral, and he recognized Corey immediately.

A faint poke of compassion had him shutting the laptop. She wasn't much older than he had been when his mother had gone.

It didn't seem right checking out photos of the wreckage of the plane, having had their son at his door only a few minutes ago.

"How does he know my real name?" Daniel said out loud and startled himself with the noise of it. *Idiot.*

His memories and coping mechanisms were so intricately woven into his emotional DNA that he sometimes felt as if they controlled him and kept him in his own world. The self-doubt and the suffocating shame were enough to hold him prisoner at times. If he let them.

*Fucking pull yourself together, you idiot. You're a strong man. No one can hurt you now.*

Yeah, he had to know what was happening here. How did this stranger from Dallas know his last name? The thought of Texas sent shivers down his spine. Was Corey something to do with what happened at Bar Five? Was he going to hurt Daniel?

*That is where they hurt you. That is where you were a real prisoner.*


Everything seemed so normal when he crossed the square. The day was cooler than usual for late spring in Denver, but as he stepped out, he welcomed the freshness on his skin. He concentrated on each step, feeling every muscle stretch and relax, and the soft grass underfoot. Students filled the benches, including the one he called *his*, a lot of them with textbooks open, some playing games or texting, and he had to dodge two bicycles to make it across the space alive.

He focused in on himself, then outward to how the world around him felt, and keeping that concentration tight, so he didn't lose control and sat on the nearest bench, refusing to move.

Corey probably wouldn't be in Hills Beans anyway, it had been at least two hours, or more, since the man had knocked on Daniel's door.

The clock in the science building showed it was nearly twelve, the sun poking through the clouds. He was hungry, and if, when he got there, Corey had gone, then maybe he'd treat himself to a much cheaper coffee at the student stand before going back to his room to eat yogurt. He'd already lost the morning, and that put him behind, so he had one hell of a lot to do to get back up to speed.

He didn't hesitate outside the hotel, walking directly through the exterior door and into the café itself. He pushed his way in and scanned the shop, expecting to find no sign of the dark-haired man who'd been at his door.

Walking into the Hills Beans Coffee Shop was like stepping out of chaos and into calm. Students didn't come in here, merely surged past the windows, everyone in a desperate hurry to be somewhere, but in here, it was quiet and still and smelled of rich coffee and pastries.

Unfortunately, even though the café was nearly empty, one of the few people in there was Corey and another man with his back to Daniel. They were talking soft and low, leaning into each other. Corey glanced at the door opening and pushed himself from his table, stalking over to Daniel with purpose. In defense, Daniel took a step back from Corey, but Corey stopped before he reached him.

"Sorry, I didn't think," Corey apologized.

"Think about what?"

"Scaring you, getting too close so fast…" Corey blinked at him, opened and shut his mouth a few times as if he had a lot more to say and didn't know how to phrase the words. Then he shook his head.

"Ignore me. I'm so pleased you're here, Daniel. Do you remember Jack?"

Daniel peered past Corey at the man who stood by the table, his fingers hooked into his belt loops and impossibly bright blue eyes focused intently on him.

Of course, Daniel knew Jack. The question was, why was Jack Campbell-Hayes waiting for him with this crazy Corey guy? Fear lodged in his throat that this was something terrible, some dark shadow that would finally take him down.

"I know who he is," he said.

Sick and shaky, Daniel couldn't move, but Corey was talking to him as if seeing this specter from his past wasn't killing Daniel slowly. He'd never wanted anything more to do with Jack, or what he'd stood for, or to even think about his old life. He took a single step backward, heading for the door without taking his gaze from the big cowboy, and Jack closed his eyes briefly, as if he was scared to see Daniel run from him.

"Please stay," he heard Jack say, and the memory of his voice snapped his eyes open. Jack stared right at him, his expression raw. Daniel couldn't move. He was frozen to the spot. Fearfully, he checked the corners of the cozy coffee shop with its dark sofas and highly polished metalwork. This place was out of his comfort zone, not a safe place he'd checked out, and his earlier bravado had left him.

Were others here waiting in the shadows? Jack had seemed like an okay guy, thoughtful, compassionate, and Liam, another victim, had gone to him for support. Trusted him. But that didn't mean he didn't have friends who might want to hurt Daniel.

After all, Daniel had trusted Frank, with his dog collar and his perfect family, and look where that had gotten him.

"Would you like a drink?" Corey asked.

"Huh?"

"Coffee? Would you like some? I can't have anymore. I've had five, and I'm shaking."

Daniel stared at Corey who continued to talk *at* him. He'd said something about having too much coffee, holding out a hand to indicate the shakiness, but Daniel could already see Corey's intense wide-eyed focus, indicative of someone who had consumed too much caffeine.

"What is he doing here? Who are you?" Daniel thumbed at Jack and took another step away, the shop door firm against his shoulders. It didn't matter that he was blocking the doorway. Anyone trying to get through would find they couldn't. He was aware other patrons were studying him with curiosity, but he ignored them. He was used to being stared at, and after all these years, he had found a place in his head where he didn't really care. The big man was a fish out of the water, all denim and plaid, worn and sturdy, in a place where skinny, thoughtful, prideful academics and worried parents usually sat. There was nothing academic about Jack. He was focus and dignity and resolve all wrapped up into one strong package, and he was the same as he had been at the trial. Larger than life.

As if he knew what was going through Daniel's mind, he sat down again, appearing less imposing than when he was standing.

"You're safe here," Jack said. "I won't let anything hurt you."

"Nothing is hurting me right now, and if I walk out, nothing will." That was more bravado than he thought he was capable of.

Corey glanced at Jack, then sighed heavily. "He's part of this, Daniel, and he wants to advocate for you, and I needed him here, so it's my fault, and I'm sorry if this is too much." Corey held out a hand in entreaty and was so calm and in control. "I just want to talk to you."

Daniel gripped the handle behind him.

"What if I don't want to talk?" Daniel snapped and gripped the handle even tighter. The barista was staring at them. Why was the shop so fucking quiet? He glanced at the two tables that held people, and they seemed to sense something was wrong, both small groups hurrying to leave out of the other door which went straight into the hotel. At least the barista stayed. Corey was a slender, shorter guy who Daniel could handle, and the lobby was right behind him if he needed to get away from Jack or call for help.

*Scream for help.*

"I want to ask you some questions. Would you like coffee?" Corey asked.

Daniel could turn and leave now. He didn't want to think about his past, didn't want it touching the safe, or at least mostly safe, world he'd created here.

At college, he was Daniel Brown, not Daniel Chandler,

and he was the quiet, conscientious loner who everyone stared at and talked about, but no one bothered.

Apart from G on the bench in the mornings.

That was the way he liked it.

When night terrors of faceless men holding him down and hurting him woke him, or when he couldn't escape and everything was lost, he had become used to putting that dread into a box. Rarely did it appear in daylight, and during those times, he'd hidden away in his room.

But seeing Jack here? He could feel the box lid begin to slide, and he was petrified of what he might need to confront.

*No one can hurt you now. No one wants you to take the stand against a murdering abuser. He's dead. The rest are in prison.*

"Just one drink. I promise you, I'm not here to hurt you, and neither is Jack."

"Then why *are* you here?"

The question seemed to throw Corey as if he hadn't expected to have to talk at the door, almost like he had a moment fixed in his head to talk to Daniel and this wasn't that time. He looked vulnerable, scared, and as emotionally out of his depth as Daniel. That much was clear.

Maybe it wouldn't hurt to listen to what they had to say? Corey had already begun to lose his grip, and the hateful self-destructive part of him that craved confronting what he'd done in the past urged him to listen.

Jack had always shown a particular kind of gruff kindness, and Corey held so much pain in his expression. What could they do to him here in public?

*They want you to focus on the past. They want you to*

*remember what Hank Castille did to you, what the other men paid to do to you. Jack and Corey want you to wake up tonight sobbing in fear, wrapped in sheets so tight that you can't escape. They want you to hurt.*

He thought back to Doctor Greenway and her advice that the past was done and it was a person move on from it, accept it, that made it stay there. His psychologist was a big believer in processing and accepting and believing and moving on, but how could Daniel ever honestly do any of that when the night terrors slipped into daylight hours?

"Please," Corey murmured, so quietly that Daniel had to strain to hear.

"Water," Daniel finally decided. "Five minutes and I'm gone."

"Thank you." Corey bounced on his toes briefly as if the weight had lifted from his shoulders and he'd lost the ability to stay fixed to the ground. "Have a seat. Are you hungry?" He patted his belly. "I think I need to eat something, to soak up the coffee."

Great, now he was being polite and acting as if Daniel was his damn friend and they were here to catch up on the news. No fucking way.

"No, I won't be staying long enough to eat."

For a second the pain was back in Corey's eyes as he stared at Daniel, and there was that hurt and confusion in his expression. He didn't vocalize the emotions, just gestured to the table where Jack was, silently asking for Daniel to sit. Then, he hurried to the counter and ordered water coffee and whatever else he was getting. Daniel went to the table and took Corey's seat, with his back to the wall so he could look out, and people watch.

"Daniel, it's good to see you again," Jack said, extending his hand.

Daniel shook his hand but didn't linger with the touch. He couldn't say he was pleased to see Jack, so he said nothing at all. Jack had tried to contact him a couple of times. So had Darren Castille. But he had nothing to say to either of them really, and he didn't need anyone in his life so intrinsically tied to what he'd been through.

Jack was a nice enough man, all confident and powerful. Someone who got things done and wasn't fazed by silly things like fear or panic. Daniel was going to be like that one day.

Corey was quickly back, with the water coffees and creamer on a tray.

"I ordered a load of food in case you feel like eating something."

"I won't."

It wasn't that he was being stubborn, or even that he wanted to walk out right at this moment, but Daniel hated the thought of someone else getting him food he hadn't considered eating. Christ knew where that hang-up came from, but the struggle was real, not to mention he felt lightheaded and sick.

He concentrated on his water, checking that it was sealed, then opening the cap and staring at it without drinking it, waiting for whatever Corey and Jack were here to say. He could anticipate this as being *excellent* water, knowing it probably cost five bucks, and that was the only thing he could focus on.

"You must have questions?" Corey asked.

"Apart from the one about why you're here, what Jack

Campbell-Hayes is doing here, and also why the hell are you using my birth name?"

He couldn't believe he'd actually strung those words together in a coherent sentence. Hell, anyone passing would think he sounded in control of everything.

"I'm here to make sure you don't get hurt," Jack said, his tone like whiskey over ice, his blue eyes clear of deceit.

"Corey says you're my advocate."

Jack nodded. "Always."

"What does that even mean for me?" Daniel waited for Jack to explain how he was protecting Daniel's interests, or defending him, or making sure that Daniel was going to be okay, but Jack suddenly looked so fierce.

"Anyone messes with you, and I'll be right there in your corner," he said, his voice like steel. The focus and intent of the words didn't sit well with Daniel. He'd never had anyone who would be a barrier to the outside world, and he wasn't sure it would be starting now.

Daniel turned to Corey. "So I take it from that Corey is here to hurt me, then."

Corey shook his head, but his expression betrayed him, the guilt carved into every line.

Daniel braced himself for the pain, knowing it was exactly eight steps to the door.

Just in case he wanted to run.

## Chapter Four

CHAPTER FOUR. DANIEL'S WORDS SPUN IN HIS HEAD.
*You're here to hurt me, then.*

He didn't want to hurt Daniel any more than he wanted to hurt anyone. He wasn't the kind of person who went around destroying other people's lives. Daniel was tired, worn down, his dark eyes filled with pain, and for the first time, Corey regretted starting any of this.

*He deserves to know; he deserves compensation. I need to understand why my parents died and I have to protect my sisters.*

The only issue was that now they were here, with Jack insisting on attending, Corey didn't know what to say or at least where to start.

"I guess you looked up the stories about my parents?"

"I did." Something flashed in Daniel's expression. Compassion maybe?

Corey paused before leaning forward. "My uncle, as well. Did you read about him? Did you see his photo?"

"I did. Is that the question you want to ask because it's pretty fucking lame."

He and Jack exchanged glances. "Did you recognize him?"

Daniel frowned, and the corner of his mouth lifted a little as he thought. "Not at all. Your dad and uncle don't even look like brothers. That's all I thought."

"Uncle Drake was actually adopted as a baby." Corey sat back in his chair and exhaled noisily. A tiny part of him had hoped that he wouldn't have to explain, like maybe there was even a chance that Daniel could bring answers to the table. Of the other three boys, Liam, Kyle, and Gabriel, only Gabriel had recognized Drake, but that was from the hotels he used to work in, not from what had happened at the Bar Five.

"Shit," he said and closed his eyes briefly.

"What? Why are you here, Corey? What do you want from me?" Daniel was irritable and confused, and Corey was knocked back with a combination of guilt and fear and was abruptly lost for words.

The hesitation was enough for Daniel to push his water away as if he was leaving. "This is bullshit."

Corey reached over and placed a hand on his. "Daniel, I'm here because we need to talk. At least I think we do. My uncle... Drake Dryden, do you really not recognize him at all?"

Daniel shook his head. "I never even saw the man in my life. Why are you asking me that? Is this something to do with Bar Five? I won't talk through that again with anyone. Especially not in a fucking coffee shop in full public view." There was anger and fear now in Daniel's expression. All Corey could think was how much of what happened to him had Daniel tried to forget?

Was Drake's face one of those things he'd chosen to block out. Or had Corey's father been wrong? Was it possible that Drake had nothing to do with what had happened to Daniel? Now Corey felt more than uneasy. Fear curled inside him, and he wanted to leave just as much as Daniel did.

"We think... no, we know... that is, I know... Jack, I don't know where to start."

Jack twisted his coffee mug on the table, staring down at it. "From the beginning," he suggested. There was something so reassuringly firm about Jack, a man who Corey had come to know quite well over the past three months. He and Riley were solid with their support and friendship, and they took what happened with Hank Castille very seriously. They'd been his support for ninety days, made him see that what his uncle had done hadn't been anything to do with him. When he'd said he wanted to talk to Daniel, Jack had insisted on coming with him, to advocate for Daniel but also to be there for Corey.

Was it wrong to respect Jack as a kind of father figure? He was only fifteen years older than Corey, but he was so in control as if somehow he had knowledge of the universe and his place in it. Not just that, but he'd spent so much time talking to Corey, allowing him to make sense of the things he'd found out. Him, his husband Riley, and Liam who had the same haunted look in his eyes as Daniel did.

"Drake Dryden was a friend of... wait" Corey scrubbed at his eyes, knowing that it was vital he got this right. Then he lowered his voice. "I need to go back to the beginning of what I know. My father, Edward Dryden, hired an investigator after being advised about four years ago by his accountants, that money was being embezzled from the company. Not huge amounts, something that had raised no red flags for a long time. His own brother, my uncle, stole hundreds of thousands of dollars from the company and our family. Only, it wasn't just the embezzling that was found, but much more information came out about my uncle, like his family tree. He was related to a man who had died in prison. You know him. Yuri Fensen."

"Yuri."

Daniel was pale, his hands shaky as he gripped his water.

"They were cousins, and Yuri was the man who—"

"I know who he is. I know all the names and faces of the men I actually saw. You don't have to explain to me who the fuck they are."

Corey should have stopped then, but he had something to say, and even though his rational brain knew he could hurt Daniel, he had to make sure if Daniel knew anything.

He was desperate for some reason why the plane crash had happened. Something that meant his father hadn't deliberately flown the plane into solid rock and left his children without parents.

"What do you mean by the ones you saw? Did things happen when you didn't see faces?" He knew he was fucking this up. That was a horrific thing to ask a man who'd suffered abuse as Daniel had. Daniel could have been unconscious, drugged. Who knew what kind of hell he'd been through?

*You know the hell. You've seen photos of some of the others.*

"Corey," Jack cautioned.

Corey couldn't ignore Jack's warning or the guilt he felt at blurting out something so raw. "I'm sorry. This isn't me. I don't know what is going on in my head. Ignore I asked that." He ran his fingers through his hair and gripped the length of it. So many questions he had to ask that he held back because, despite that crass question, he wasn't a complete asshole.

"How the hell do you want me to forget you asked that?" Daniel stood so fast his chair slammed back to the wall with a crash. "I can't tell you I knew all of them, or that I even know how many different men used me or how often." His tone was low, but the agony in each word cut Corey to the bone.

Corey stood as well. "Shit. No, please, I didn't mean—"

"There were too many to list," Daniel snapped, sweeping his hand across the table and knocking over his water. "Men with faces twisted in lust, some in masks, men who paid to be with me, people who Yuri and Hank owed money to, but no, I didn't see all their faces. Does that answer your question?"

"Masks," Corey repeated brokenly, realization flooding him, pain cutting into his heart. That would explain things like why no one knew his uncle had been any part of this. Then that same realization and fear made him blurt out things he shouldn't have said. Words he wished he could pull back as soon as they left his mouth. "Why didn't any of you mention this at the trial? I've seen the transcripts, and you didn't say anything about masks—"

"Corey, that's enough," Jack ordered as Daniel recoiled

at the accusations and anger in Corey's voice. *Shit. Why am I so fucking stupid? What am I doing? This isn't me.*

"Fuck you. Both of you," Daniel said, his voice shaky, his hands in fists, and his skin pale.

Jack stood and immediately moved between them with his back to Corey. He couldn't see Jack's expression, but his tone was soft.

"Can we take this somewhere else? Somewhere private. I have a suite. It's big, and you can trust me to look after you. There are things we think you should know."

Daniel didn't answer him at first, but Corey stayed quiet as remorse stole his words. Grief and misery and hatred for what his family had done to Daniel gripped him, and he couldn't breathe.

Corey stepped closer. "Shit, Daniel, I'm sorry."

Daniel wasn't listening. He was backing away, and Corey was going to lose the chance to talk to him.

"Please don't go, Daniel. I'm sorry. I can do better."

"Let him be." Jack gripped Corey's arm, but all Corey wanted to do was reach out and hug Daniel. Touch him and reassure him that he hadn't meant to scrape off the scabs of old wounds so brutally. Then Jack was talking to Daniel, "We're in the Mountain Suite until lunchtime tomorrow. There will be a card in the name of Daniel Brown at reception for the elevator. Will you come and find us?"

Daniel shook his head and then vanished.

"Fuck, Jack, what did I do?" He was close to losing his mind, but the reassuring press of Jack's hand on his shoulder was enough for him to stop wanting to run after Daniel.

"This is all too raw; for both of you," Jack stated. "We're going back to the suite, and we will wait to see if he comes to us, and if he doesn't, then you'll go back to Dallas, and you'll have to forget you ever met him, as you said you would."

Corey didn't want to hear that. He'd pushed Daniel too far, but he had his sisters to think about. His father being held responsible for orchestrating a deliberate murder-suicide, which was what the press and the crash investigators had hinted at, would destroy his sisters.

"My family, Jack. I can't let this hurt my sisters."

Jack softened a little and cupped Corey's shoulder again. "I know, Corey, but what Daniel has been through, what drove Kyle and Gabriel to Legacy, and what makes Liam fight depression and anxiety? That is still inside Daniel, and he's got to be terrified. You might not find your answers here. Maybe you shouldn't have even looked."

Jack hadn't thought this was a good idea. No one had.

*Why didn't I listen? What the hell am I trying to do?*

Corey nodded, even though his heart was cracking. He'd held hope that Daniel would have answers, and he'd pushed too hard, scared him into running off. But he couldn't go after him. He wasn't that kind of person.

He and Jack made their way to the suite, the elevator slow, stopping at almost every floor until finally, it opened on seventeen.

"I fucked up," Corey said, tired and miserable and out of his depth.

Jack shrugged. "You're hurting as well, just in a different way."

"I didn't mean to say all that," Corey admitted and

waited for Jack to say it was okay, that he understood why Corey had lost track of his mind for the fatal few seconds. He needed someone to endorse his actions so that he didn't feel like a spineless fool who hurt people all the time.

"I know," Jack began, but then he sighed. "You promised me you'd go slow, Corey. You can't lay all that on Daniel without thinking about what it would do to the kid."

Weird that all Corey said was entirely off in a new direction, when all he could think about was Jack's description of Daniel as a kid. "He was twenty-two a month ago, so he's a grown man."

"What?" Jack asked, confused.

"You called him a kid, and he's not. He's twenty-two."

Jack shook his head, sadly. "He'll always be a kid to me. When I remember the courtroom, all I see is a young kid, shaking so hard as he talked that sometimes you couldn't hear the words clearly. He was the last of them, we think. The youngest."

Corey groaned. "I can't believe I said that about my uncle. Why would Daniel know him? It might not have been him that Drake even went near."

The words didn't need a reply. Corey wanted Jack's respect, but he'd not done anything today to deserve it.

"Maybe you should go home and leave this now," Jack observed.

Fear spiked in Corey. He didn't want to leave. He had his sisters to think about. He didn't care about himself, but his sisters were his whole life now. He had to be hard, and focused, and push aside his natural tendency to see every situation from all sides.

He had to ignore the strength that had gotten him this

far, ignore his compassion and trust. Anything to find out what had really happened on that plane.

"I'd do anything for the people I love," Corey said.

Jack nodded. "I know, Corey. Believe me. I'm the same."

Corey split off to his own room, closing the door and slumping onto the bed. When the PI had tracked Daniel down, Corey hadn't been able to take it all in.

But right now he needed answers, and Daniel was his only chance of letting his parents rest in peace.

And keeping his sisters safe.

## Chapter Five

DANIEL WATCHED THE TWO MEN GO INTO THE ELEVATOR from his position behind a marble column by the reception. No one came to talk to him or tell him to move on, and he waited until the doors had closed before straightening and then walking out into the fresh air of a spring Denver afternoon.

He was confused and angry and wasn't sure which emotion he should let dominate his thoughts. How dare they come into his ordered life and start asking questions about something he'd hidden away? Who the hell did they think they were?

*I need to leave. Go back to my room. Push everything into a box.*

But what did Corey mean about an uncle? Why was it so crucial whether Daniel recalled him, and why did Corey's expression hold so much pain? Was it possible that Corey was another one of the lost boys? Had his uncle hurt him? The article that Daniel read had said Corey had three sisters, the youngest only six. Were they victims as well?

His head pounded, the noise unbearable, and the fresh air helped only to clear his thoughts enough to know that he was curious about what they wanted him to hear. Was it curiosity? Or fear? His therapist had said that he should face up to things on his own terms, but he hadn't actually faced up to anything at all.

*Three more weeks. One more exam. Then I have to face up to the real world whether I like it or not.*

"You okay?" someone asked him, and he blinked at a skinny girl with purple hair and so many piercings he couldn't count them all. She had a hand on his arm and questions on her face.

"Of course," Daniel answered by rote. That was his standard reply.

"Do you have low sugar? Are you diabetic?"

"What?"

"Do you want me to call 911?" Then she was talking to someone else. "I think he's ill."

The question made no sense, and then he realized where he was; right in the middle of the fucking road with cars stopping behind him. The cacophony in his head that wouldn't end was horns and shouting, not his memories running him down.

"Shit, I'm okay, sorry." He moved out of the road and sat on the bench on the sidewalk, purple-haired girl following him.

"You sure you're going to be okay?" She had pretty violet eyes.

He forced a smile. "Exam stress."

She was instantly relieved. "Oh God, I know. I have Poli-Sci exams tomorrow, and it's killing me."

"Thanks for your help," he said. "I'm good. I just spaced out."

She handed him a water bottle and then sketched a wave. "Good luck in your exams."

He waited until she left and then stood before tossing the bottle into the trash.

"No more fucking running," he said to himself, his hands in fists. He returned to the hotel, realizing he'd nearly made it halfway back to his dorm in a fugue-like state. One day the mess in his head was going to kill him. He went straight up to reception.

"My name is Daniel Brown." He passed over his ID. "You have a card for me?"

The receptionist smiled at him, checked the ID, and returned it with an envelope. "Seventeenth floor, sir."

"Can I use this card to get on that floor if I take the stairs?"

"You can, but it's a long way up." She laughed as if maybe she thought he was making a joke? Nope. This was no joke.

"It's fine, thank you," he said and left before he was put in a position to explain why he would rather manage all those flights than use an elevator.

When he reached the right place, the door with a security pad indicating this was an area with cameras, he hesitated a moment before swiping the card. He'd stopped a couple of times on the way up to catch his breath, but this stop was just to give himself a little thinking time, focusing on Corey and whatever the man was hiding behind his green eyes.

The door swung open and onto a wide hallway with only two doors, and he headed for the one with the sign for the Mountain Suite, a cute artsy plaque with snowcapped mountains as a backdrop. Then he knocked.

Jack answered the door.

"Daniel—"

"Corey obviously has things to say. I don't know if I need to hear them and whatever the hell is going on here, but I'll listen, and then you make him leave me alone."

Jack stepped back, letting Daniel in.

"You don't have to do this," Jack explained, and for a moment Daniel allowed himself to think he could run. Then he straightened, pushed his shoulders back, and walked in.

"Where is he?"

"I'm here," Corey said from the doorway of another room inside. He looked so damn grateful. "Thank you for coming back."

*Stay focused.*

Daniel stood his ground. "Mr. Campbell-Hayes, you need to leave."

"Jack, please. Also, I'm not going anywhere."

"Yes, you are. I'm getting half the story with you advocating for me, or whatever shit you have going on. No disrespect, but I don't need anyone supporting me."

"Daniel—"

"I'm not messing here, *Jack*. I'm not a kid."

Jack glanced from Daniel to Corey, then sighed. "I'll be in my room." Before Daniel could argue that this wasn't exactly what he meant by Jack leaving, he took another door and closed it behind him.

Daniel rounded on Corey immediately. "Start from the beginning. Why did you find me? What do you want to ask me about this uncle of yours? You have ten minutes. and then I'm gone."

Corey nodded and hovered where he was, and Daniel waited for him to start talking. The moment he'd reached his fill of staring at Corey was the point when Corey found his words.

"One hundred and eleven days ago I lost my parents, and that is the only place I know where to start."

Daniel leaned back on the nearest wall and waited for more. Corey crossed to a sofa, sitting on the very edge of it.

"The plane they were in, a small jet that was owned by our company, piloted by my dad, crashed into a mountain. It was clear, dry. There were no side winds, They were off-course, but not by a lot. There were no reported prior mechanical issues or messages of distress. They simply flew directly into a mountainside and disappeared from traffic control screens. Their flight plan showed they were heading for Denver. Something backed up by a note in my dad's journal. When the first responders reached the plane, there was nothing left except twisted, burned wreckage, and nothing left of my parents that we could bury suitably."

Compassion nudged at Daniel, and he pushed off from the wall and sat on a chair opposite Corey.

Corey continued, his expression was unfocused. "They found the flight recorder. There was what the experts called an altercation in the cockpit, but they haven't made that public yet, although it will only be a matter of days. They couldn't make much out, but my uncle was shouting. Then the plane fell from the sky. They never found out where my mom was in all of this." He paused and settled his breathing, which had quickened as the words spilled out of him. Daniel could see the effort he was making to stay in control, but Corey's grasp of it was slipping.

"I'm sorry for your parents dying," Daniel murmured, and he meant it. He'd lost people, seen death, and he'd mourned those losses at the time.

Corey nodded slightly, acknowledging the words, although Daniel was sure he'd heard them a lot so far.

"My dad kept journals, and when I was going through his things, I found a letter from a private investigation agency. Confirmation, with photos, of horrible crimes that were possibly connected to my uncle. The same man who used to spoil my sisters and me. The same man I thought I loved like an uncle. The one who it turned out was a potential pedophile and abuser and was part of what happened at the Bar Five, and to you, maybe."

"You know this for sure?"

*Is it just me, or is my voice shaky?*

"It's what the PI says, what's in my dad's journal, but I don't have any other proof."

"Maybe your dad was wrong."

Corey stiffened. "My dad was a good man—"

"Whatever. As I said before, I don't recognize your uncle or his eyes." Daniel knew that statement would confuse Corey, but Corey was intent on pressing ahead. He was a handsome man, slim, short, his dark hair soft and in long layers, his eyes a deep mossy green that changed color with his emotions. Daniel recognized something of himself in Corey, in that cautious way he controlled himself. But the rest, the wild passion that Daniel had seen in him in the coffee shop made him wary because it could slip out at any point.

"I know you said that, but you're my last hope. The others don't know him. Liam, Gabriel, Kyle. So if none of you know him, did he do what my dad said he did? Did he confront my uncle on that plane? Was that the reason for the fight and the crash? And why were they going to Denver? Was it to find you? Why didn't they talk to the others first? What was it about you, or Denver, that was so special? I want to understand so that I can give my sisters a reason for everything so that the ghosts of our family's past don't rear up and destroy their futures."

"What were you planning on doing if I had recognized him? Make me write a statement? Make me tell the world again exactly what happened to me?"

"No, yes, I don't fucking know what I want to do. Protect my sisters. That's all."

"You don't need me to pass over suspicions to the authorities. Why don't you just take what your dad wrote and give it to the cops?"

Corey dropped his head and exhaled. "Because I met Jack and Liam. Kyle. Gabriel. I won't do that to them or to you. They're good people, and unless I had to…" He scrubbed at his eyes again. "What do I do? What if the rumors that say my dad killed my mom and my uncle deliberately are true? What if they never find out what caused the crash?"

"What do you want me to say?"

"Nothing, fuck… Should I tell the cops, my dad said these things about my uncle, pull it all through the courts, drag these people I know now, through the system again? What would it prove? Would any of it clear my dad's name, stop him from being labeled a suicidal murderer? How can I do that to them or to you?" His voice hitched as if he was fighting tears, his eyes bright, his hands in fists in his lap.

"Corey—"

"I don't even know you," he interrupted, "but the others told me what they'd seen and what had happened to them. Or at least Gabriel did. Kyle won't talk, and Liam just sat and held his boyfriend's hand as if it was the end of the world."

Jeez, he was so earnest, so compassionate and understanding.

Daniel laced his fingers together. "I can't tell you anything you don't already know. I was there. I was hurt. I remember Hank and a couple of other guys, and I'm done talking about it."

"Okay," Corey said, even though it wasn't okay because clearly, the ghosts he carried with him were pushing for answers. "I'm not a bad guy. I want to do what's best."

Daniel's chest tightened.

"I read a quote somewhere," he said, and Corey looked up at him. "Oscar Wilde I think. You only see a man's true nature when he wears a mask. When the men came to me, they reveled in anonymity, and they hurt us all. I saw their eyes, filled with greed and lust and the need to inflict pain. I always remember their eyes, but your uncle? I don't see anything when I look at his face."

He felt dizzy with the memories that flooded him.

Blue eyes? He'd been the one who liked to hit Daniel. Hazel eyes? He wanted to make Daniel cry. The man with the scar under his gray eyes? He tried to humiliate Daniel to get himself off.

"I knew Yuri by face and Hank. Yuri was a broker for

our bodies with Hank, and I knew another man. He was the one who took me from the side of the road. The others I only knew by their eyes. I wish I could give you answers on whether what the PI discovered or what your dad had written, was the truth."

*At least then one of us would find peace.*

Corey pulled out his cell phone. "What about my uncle's voice? Would you maybe recognize a voice?"

"I'm not sure I want to listen to anything."

Corey held out the phone. "Just press play."

The still for the video was a frozen image of a smiling man, holding a little girl, their eyes narrowed against the bright sun.

"This is the same uncle?" He was different than the official photos in the paper, relaxed and happy. In neither picture that Daniel had seen did he look like a monster.

"From my birthday last July. He was holding my sister as if nothing was wrong. Like he wasn't someone who could have hurt kids." Corey hugged himself and closed his eyes, rocking a little. "He held my baby sister."

Daniel's thumb hovered over the triangle to play. The last cell he'd had was an old Nokia he'd owned that he'd left at his home all those years ago. That had been a clumsy brick of a thing, a secondhand cell that his cousin had given him. This was shiny and thin, and the sound when he pressed play was of Corey's sister laughing. She clung to her uncle like a monkey, her long dark hair flying out around her as he swung her. It was a pretty film to watch. A man who obviously loved his niece, and there was no hatred there. Nothing but love. He set her down, patted her head, and she giggled and ran away.

"No running around the pool!" the man on the video

shouted and then laughed at whoever was filming them. "She'll hurt herself one day."

The video ended, the still showing the laughing man and the girl again.

Daniel's hold on the phone faltered, and it slipped to the floor. The voice...

*You love me hurting you. You fucking love it.*

Then his world went black.

## Chapter Six

Corey was at his side in a second, calling for Jack and almost catching Daniel as he slipped sideways from the chair.

He'd shut down, right in front of Corey, his eyes rolling back, and he'd passed out.

Jack was there in an instant, checking his pulse and then sitting back on his haunches.

"Shit," he cursed and pressed a hand to Daniel's head. "What happened?" He looked up as he said that, and Corey cringed.

"I fucked up. He heard Drake's voice and passed out."

"Jesus, Corey."

"I know." Since he'd found those damn journals, he'd done nothing but fuck things up. He slid to his knees next to Daniel. "Do we call 911?"

Did this mean that Daniel had recognized the voice? Was this real? Had his uncle really been a monster? He curled his hand into the material of Daniel's jacket and pressed his hand to Daniel's forehead. His skin was warm and slightly damp, and Corey reached for the phone to call first responders.

Fear niggled at him that Daniel was epileptic, but what had happened hadn't been a seizure. There were no fits or movement. Only the fall of Daniel fainting dead away.

"Should I call 911?" he asked again, needing Jack's reassurance that he should do that right now.

Daniel stirred, opened his eyes, blinking, and stared up at Corey, unfocused.

"No, look, he's coming around," Jack observed and rubbed Daniel's shoulder, folding his jacket and pushing it under Daniel's head to raise it a little. "You'll be okay," he said to Daniel, and Corey didn't know what the fuck to do.

Daniel closed his eyes again, but this time he wasn't unconscious. In fact, he seemed to be sleeping as he curled into a ball on his side, pushing his face against Jack's leg.

"Daniel?" Jack spoke firmly and added a little shake of Daniel's arm to the words.

Finally, Daniel opened his eyes, looking up at them both and frowning.

"Wha'appened?" he slurred.

"You passed out," Jack said.

Daniel groaned, louder this time, and shut his eyes again. "Shit, shit, fuck, shit," he cursed, his fists clenching and banging on his hips in time with the curses. Then in a smooth move that belied his size and his recent lack of consciousness, he rolled to a sitting position and bent his head.

"Can I get you something? Water, or…?" Corey didn't know what to do for the best. Was coffee maybe what Daniel needed to give his system a snap start, or was water the thing to give him? He looked to Jack who shook his head subtly.

Daniel shook his head. "Air," he murmured and stood shakily. Corey held out a hand to help, but Daniel sidestepped him and stumbled, not to the door into the apartment, but to the nearest source of fresh air, the balcony. He tried the handle, and Corey hurried over.

"Why is it locked? Why have you locked me in? What the fuck is happening?" His words tumbled out in a mess of fear and temper, and Corey quickly unlocked the door. Daniel fell out onto the balcony, faltering to a stop, bent at the waist, with his hands on his knees. Corey went to his side instinctively, and Jack was right behind, positioning himself between Daniel and the wrought iron railings that edged the balcony.

"I'm so sorry," Corey blurted, needing to know that Daniel understood that for the most selfish of reasons.

Daniel shrugged him off and moved to the small bench to one side, sitting absolutely still. Corey followed him, but Jack waited and watched.

"Does that kind of thing happen often?" Corey kept the question soft and bumped elbows with Daniel, who inched away from him.

"Not for a long time." He sighed heavily before sitting upright. "Your uncle. I don't know his face, but I recognized his voice." He leaned over again, a hand over his mouth as if he was going to be sick.

"You listened, and what happened? What did you hear…? Was he one of the ones who…?"

*Why can't I get my words out properly?*

Now it was Daniel's turn to talk, but he was quiet for the longest time, and still, Jack didn't move from his spot.

"What do you want me to say? Our lawyer convinced me that if I said anything about masked men, it would be… God, I can't even remember much of what he said. He wanted it cut and dried, no room for misinterpretation, so we concentrated on *them*." Unspoken were the names Hank Castille and Yuri Fensen. "But I will never forget the eyes of the men who hurt me, the ones I could see, but your uncle? I remember his voice. He liked to …" He stopped and stared at Corey, and Corey knew that Daniel didn't want to say, and he wasn't going to push it.

"God, I'm so sorry." Corey's world was disintegrating around him. Part of him had hoped that what his dad had been told wasn't right. But he'd hurt Daniel, and that was the last thing he should have done. Daniel looked as if he could handle anything, but that wasn't true.

Daniel's hand was in his lap, and Corey reached over to touch it, shocked when Daniel curled his fingers up and held Corey's hand for the briefest of moments.

"It's okay," Daniel murmured and moved away from Corey. It sounded as if he was trying to reassure Corey and himself at the same time.

They sat in silence for a few moments.

Finally, Corey vocalized what he was thinking. "I have to decide what to do about Uncle Drake now. Drake, I mean. He's not any kind of uncle I want or need."

Daniel side-eyed him. "What do you mean 'decide'?"

"I don't know what I mean."

*How's that for honesty?*

"He's dead, and I have nothing else to say," Daniel snapped. "Whatever the hell you think you are deciding to do, I won't ever revisit what Daniel Chandler saw or did."

Corey was horrified that Daniel thought he would

make him do that. "No, I mean, compensation, you and the others, my uncle's estate. I want you and the others to have the money—"

Daniel stood up, shaky, holding a hand out to stop Corey from talking. "What? This is about money? You want to pay us all to stay quiet? Believe me, there isn't any amount of money that will make me say a fucking thing."

"No, I don't mean to pay you off. Jesus—"

"Give the money to the others. I've already taken blood money once, and I won't do it again."

"Daniel, one of my family hurt you, and I want to make it right."

Daniel shook his head. "Money won't fix my nightmares." Then without another word, he walked away from Corey and left him sitting on the balcony bench, as the suite door shut and he'd gone.

"He's right. Money doesn't solve everything." Jack was gruff, his voice thick with emotion. "When you think what those boys went through you wouldn't even think that it could."

Corey rounded on the man he'd come to respect. "I wasn't trying to pay him off or think money will help. I just want to make things right, for me, for my family. We need a nondisclosure, to make financial reparations. I have to protect my sisters."

Jack hooked his thumbs into his belt.

"You can't pay someone to make them hide their pain, and shit, Corey, secrets never end well."

Shame flooded Corey. Was his family more important than understanding what Daniel was going through? Daniel held secrets that could destroy him and his sisters. He didn't care about himself, but Amy, Chloe, and

Sophie? That was a different story. But did that make this right?

"Jack, what am I doing? Why am I still here? I need to go and talk to him," he said, but Jack stopped him. "I have to make sure he's okay. Someone who hurts people like this? I'm not my uncle. I'm not that man."

"I'll go. Stay here."

So Corey stayed. His guilt was too heavy for him to hold the weight of it, so he remained on the bench and stared out at the mountains and hated himself with every breath.

Could he really hurt someone to keep his family safe? Was that what he'd been doing? Trying to pay Daniel to stay quiet?

***

Daniel made it down the stairs to the mezzanine. He wasn't ready to go down into the lobby, not able to face people just now. He'd taken money before, and it had destroyed him, but he had a degree now, or at least he nearly had one. He was an athlete, a scholarship student, a man who knew that he wanted to find somewhere else to make his life. He wasn't far enough away from Texas and had applied for business internships in states that were as far away from Texas as he could get.

Nothing had panned out yet as his academic levels weren't excellent, probably because he'd lost a lot of time to being fucked in the head. Too many migraines, too many panic attacks, but somehow he'd scraped through his degree, and that meant *something*.

He wasn't stupid. He wasn't a kid. Things in his head

had cracked wide open since watching that video. He settled his breathing, leaning against the wall in a dark corner, and as soon as he had full control, he took the final few stairs to the exit; coming face-to-face with Jack.

"What?" he asked, tired of everything today.

"You remember Darren and I said I'd do anything to help you if you ever needed it, the same as Darren did?"

Daniel remembered Darren, the brother of Hank Castille. The one who'd sent him the check from proceeds of the sale of Bar Five.

*Blood money.*

There had been a covering letter explaining that he'd always be there for Daniel if needed.

Everyone seemed to think that money and offers to help solved all the problems.

"I need to go." He bypassed Jack, who made no effort to stop him.

"Corey's a good guy really. He's grieving and lost and lashing out at anything that may hurt his family."

The words made Daniel stop, and he spun to face Jack.

"Well, he hurt me," Daniel snapped.

Jack nodded and sighed. "I know, and I wanted to stop him. I could have stopped him, and I owe you an apology for failing on both counts." He held out a piece of paper. It looked like hotel stationery from the emblem at the top. "Kyle has a home with us at a place called Legacy Ranch, and Gabriel spends a lot of time there, working with the kids who come through to them."

Daniel didn't take the paper. "I'm not a fucking charity case. I'm making something of myself on my own terms, and I don't need a handout to make things seem better."

He was trying his hardest to get Jack to back off, but

the words didn't hit their intended mark as Jack ignored his impassioned speech and forged ahead.

"Kyle works for Legacy ranch. It's a place for disenfranchised kids who need a place to stay."

"I'm not a fucking kid," Daniel shouted.

"No, you're not. Legacy Ranch could do with a business manager, and hell, maybe you would fit in there, or maybe you wouldn't. Your degree is in business, right? When you finish it, you could do big things, and the opportunity is there for you. Visit, talk to Kyle, meet Gabriel again, find out what it took for him to survive, have a place with them, and the horses, and the people that they help. Liam is there as well. He manages the place, or at least he did until Kyle took over. Don't waste your talents on some Fortune 500 company that sticks you in a post room for ten years. Work at Legacy."

"I said I don't need your help."

Jack shook the paper a little, and Daniel finally took it, folding it and pushing it into his pocket.

"I won't go to this Legacy place."

"Promise me you'll think about it?"

Daniel left before he crumbled and caved and allowed other people to take care of him.

This was his life now, and he wasn't going to let it destroy him. He was going to make himself into a new man, and he didn't need any help with that.

## Chapter Seven

**Six months later**

DANIEL INCHED FORWARD TO LOOK BETWEEN THE SEATS AT the road ahead. The cab driver had done nothing but chat since Daniel had hailed the cab at the bus station, and now, nearly half an hour later, they were so close to the Double D ranch he could get out of the car and walk the rest of the way.

In fact, that was exactly what he wanted to do.

"You can stop here," he told the driver, who looked at him in the mirror and raised his eyebrows.

"It's the middle of nowhere," he explained as if Daniel couldn't see for himself that land stretched away either side, and the road vanished into the distance.

"Here's fine."

"Your dime." The driver pulled over at the next convenient spot and turned in his seat. "Last chance, dude. you still have a couple of miles to get where you wanted to be."

"I'll be fine." He smiled at the guy to give the impression he had total control over his decision-making and knew precisely what he was doing. He couldn't say he really didn't want to be inside a car a moment longer, that he was on the edge of panic, and needed space and room to breathe. Then he'd just come across as an idiot.

"Okay then," the driver said and turned the screen so Daniel could see the cost of the ride. He'd managed to travel most of the way by bus, but this last bit was either taxi or walk, and it wasn't as if he didn't have the money. He had most of his salary for the previous three months sitting in an account, but he wasn't going to spend it any time soon. As long as his rent was paid on the tiny shitty room he leased, that was all he needed.

Handing over the money was easy, seeing the worry on the driver's face was something he wanted to avoid dealing with. In a few moments, he was outside on the wayside, his bag and books with him, and his purpose set. The taxi driver cast one more thoughtful glance that was nearly a frown and then put the car in drive, made a U-turn, and headed back to the city. Cars went past. It wasn't as if the Double D was in the middle of nowhere really, but he didn't stop and look as if he might need a lift of any sort. He hoisted his book bag on his back and walked with purpose.

He'd followed this route on Google maps a hundred times. At first, it was to convince himself he didn't want anything to do with Jack Campbell-Hayes or this Legacy place. Then, after a few weeks, it had been out of curiosity, and he'd found the website for Legacy—a sad small affair that needed sprucing up and was currently little more than a page on a host site for a halfway house in the city.

Then he'd started working at a medical company in Denver exactly three months ago, working as best he could and failing miserably. He hadn't made it past the probation period, and even though he'd shown promise, their thought was that an office job wasn't for him.

They were right about that. After he'd escaped Bar Five, he'd caught up at school with a state-provided tutor in a brand-new-to-him foster home which didn't suck as much as it could have done. Then he'd applied for every scholarship he could find, until finally, Denver had an available space in a marketing course, fully funded. It wasn't as far north as he'd wanted, but it was still far enough from Texas that he felt a small measure of safety. His last schooling had been one-on-one and calm. Also, college had given him a false sense of security. It had given him the idea that he could be indoors all day, following rules, and working nine to five.

Work though, *real work,* was demands and horror and painful questions.

In an office, he had no time to go and lock himself in the restroom and manage a panic attack. It gave him no chance to stop people from touching him, asking him about his family, or his history, or why didn't he have a cell phone, or explain in great detail why it was imperative he went out drinking with them on a Friday night. Timetables at college made him remember to eat, but he didn't have that in an office where managers expected you to eat on the fly.

He'd tried so hard to be normal, and he'd failed, miserably.

Finally, he'd been told he should go, and not one part of him regretted that he'd not been able to stay.

That was the moment he looked up the Campbell-Hayes and decided that he needed to cross visiting the Legacy Ranch off his to-do list.

Google maps had shown an intriguing glimpse of gates and the logo for the Double D, and Internet research revealed the kind of men Jack and Riley were, and what kind of place Legacy was. The gates were exactly as he'd seen, wide open, with a cattle guard from one side to the other, and security cameras in several positions. He'd seen several paparazzi shots of the two men and their family, seen a video they'd made on their wedding day when same-sex marriage had been made legal, understood what they wanted to say about loving who you love.

He stopped by the camera, made sure to look directly into it, to show he was not there for nefarious reasons. Then he turned to face the long road to the ranch. He knew it wasn't possible to see anything from the road, but it seemed to take forever to get to the first bend and two smaller roads leading away from it. There were signs. To the left was the *Campbell-Hayes Horse Therapy Program*, which he knew helped kids with special needs, and adults who needed a space to find peace alongside horses.

To the right was a sign that said *Legacy Ranch.*

He could carry on to the main house, but why bother. They wouldn't want to see him, and actually, he wasn't convinced he wanted to go anyway. Legacy on the other hand? Kyle would be there, and he knew exactly what Daniel was experiencing. He *had* to know.

Kyle had been at the Bar Five. He'd been treated the same way, but he'd managed to get away. Same with the other two boys, Gabriel and Liam.

He was the only one who hadn't managed to run. He

was the boy who was so damn scared of his own shadow he'd never even contemplated running. He'd been the one who someone had rescued. At least that is what he thought had happened. A lot of that final day was lost in high fevers and pain.

The sound of hooves on the dusty road behind him made him move to the side, but he kept walking.

"Howdy," someone said, a man, with a peculiar accent, possibly Australian crossed with American? It was kind of sexy. Glancing up Daniel realized the owner of the voice was kind of hot. Daniel hurried, the weight of his bags dragging him down. He didn't want to talk to some random stranger. He wanted to see the ranch and meet Kyle.

The rider dismounted a little ahead of Daniel and waited, but he wasn't blocking Daniel's path, merely waiting for him. Daniel passed around him, and he fell into step, the big black horse patiently walking beside them.

"Name's Robbie," the man said. "Welcome to Legacy."

Daniel side-eyed him but said nothing.

"You want help with your bags?" Robbie asked, but Daniel just held them tighter. Robbie didn't insist that he knew better or push and moan about how Daniel wasn't doing what was reasonable or right. For that Daniel was grateful, and they kept walking until a low building came into sight.

"Kyle'll be in there," Robbie said, then mounted his horse, wheeled around, and trotted away.

Which left Daniel standing a couple of hundred yards from what he assumed was the Legacy building. There was a central entrance, and then left and right there were separate doors, and the yard in front was mostly silent.

*What do I say now? What do I do? Where the hell do I go?*

Daniel dropped his bags to the ground and waited for inspiration. What he should really do is grow some balls go up to the door, and knock, but he couldn't do that when his vision was spotty, and his breathing labored. He sat, right in the dust, leaned back on his bag and waited. It didn't take long to get a hold of himself, and he concentrated on his breathing because that was the only way to calm down.

No one came out to find him or happen to stop by and talk to him, everything was utterly still. Finally, he scrambled to stand, picked up his bags and walked the remaining short distance to what he imagined was the main front door. He didn't have to knock. The door opened as he drew closer, but he couldn't make out the figure in the doorway. Only that the person was big, and a guy, and that he seemed to be allowing Daniel to come to him.

Once he was close enough to check the features, he knew it was Kyle. The man hadn't changed much from the courtroom. He looked healthier, brown from the sun, and he was smiling.

Daniel stopped and stared at Kyle, waiting for the panic or the fear but feeling something other than those things. Relief maybe? Or was it that hope was flooding his body? He couldn't tell.

"Hello, Daniel." Kyle stepped out of the doorway.

"You remember who I am?" Daniel couldn't believe anyone recalled who he was from those dark days, except for Jack of course. Why would anyone recall? Why would they care?

"Do you remember me?" Kyle asked softly.

"Of course I do. You're Kyle. You're the oldest."

He tilted his head a little, but there wasn't confusion on his face. "I am, yes, and to answer your question, the four of us from Bar Five will always know each other, I think."

Daniel felt as if he should agree, but his eyes burned with emotion, and there was no fucking way he was going to lose his shit in the middle of a strange place.

"Would you like to come in?" Kyle asked. The space beyond him looked dark because the sun was behind the building, but he had nothing to fear from the man. Right? Kyle moved to one side and gestured for him to come in, but Daniel was frozen to the spot.

"Wait a minute," Kyle said after a pause, vanished inside and then came back out. "Let me show you something."

Daniel stumbled back as Kyle walked toward him but at the last moment moved past him to one end of the big accommodation block. He unlocked and opened a door and then stood back.

"This is your room for all the time you're here." He held out the key. "There's only one key, and it's yours to hold onto if you want to put your bags in there. There's a bed, a bathroom, a desk, and some closet space. You can lock your stuff away, and we can talk, or you can go in and have a shower. The windows all open a little and can be locked in place, and the room has two skylights."

"I'm not staying," Daniel murmured. This wasn't exactly true as he had nowhere else to go right now, but he'd find somewhere as soon as he got his head straight.

Kyle shrugged. "Stay as long as you want. I'd love to talk to you, find out what you've been doing, see how you managed in a world I was never quite settled in."

"Well it's plain that I didn't manage to survive on my own," Daniel snapped. "That's the whole freaking point of me scurrying here with my tail between my legs."

"Jeez, Daniel. There's no shame in wanting to find somewhere that feels right. We can't all fit everywhere. You're not here because you've failed, you're here to find answers."

Great, now tears were threatening. Kyle had been in Daniel's position. Their stories were probably different, but at the end, they'd made their way to Legacy.

"What if I can't find answers because nothing like that exists? What happened to us, what they did to us, changed me to the point that I can't even hold down a job. After all the years in college, pushing through the chaos and the fear and scraping results, what's left there for me to do now?"

Kyle tucked his thumbs into his belt loops. "I didn't have a place either. I moved from job to job, never quite fitting in, never settled, always a loner, and then I found Legacy, and it was my place to stay. The skies are big here, and there's a freedom that made me feel as if I could handle everything thrown at me."

"Yeah, yeah, whatever. Great that it worked for you, but it might not be what I need." Daniel was frustrated, and it showed in his voice. Everyone seemed to have ideas about what would fix him or about the paths he should take in life, but nothing was working or making any sense yet.

"Gabriel went back to the city. He wasn't ready to live

out here full time, but he comes back a lot and found a very different kind of peace. And Liam? He's up at the Double D, working with horses. Those were their choices, but even if you decide not to stay at Legacy, then at least this place gives you space to reflect."

That was what he needed. His head was so full of the mess and noise of his past and the chaos of his present, with no clear-cut direction in his life, that he couldn't just take a moment to stop and reason out what he wanted.

"I'd like to clean up if that's okay," Daniel decided and reached for the key, holding his palm upright so Kyle could drop it into his outstretched hand. He didn't move until Kyle was out of the way, and then he stepped quickly inside this place that was apparently his, shut the door, and locked it.

For a second he looked around him. The bed wasn't made, the bedding in a neat pile inside a transparent plastic cover. The desk was empty, a pin board above it, and the skylights allowed natural light to flood the space. He unclipped the windows and locked them in the slightly open position, then dropped his bags onto the mattress. As rooms went, it was one of the best ones he'd ever been in, reminding him of his dorm without the stupid posters and the tiny bathroom. Speaking of which, he pushed open the door in the room and found a walk-in shower, a small basin, and a toilet. There was a mirror there, a towel on a hook, and a storage cupboard that held all kinds of toiletries.

What he really wanted was a shower, to wash off the dust and the dirt, and so he could maybe have some peace. But what if Kyle had been lying? What if there *was* another key to this place? He took the desk chair and wedged it under the door handle. Satisfied that anyone trying to get in would make one hell of a lot of noise, he was happy enough to use the bathroom.

He kept the water lukewarm for a long time, and then gradually eased up the temperature, using shampoo and shower gel until he was standing in a fog of sandalwood and apple. He could think in here, the skylight open to the blue beyond, the air clean and pure, and the steam relaxing him. He let his thoughts wander, but inevitable he found himself thinking about the Dryden family.

And mostly about dark-haired, green-eyed, confusing, gorgeous hurtful Corey.

Corey had rocked something in him, with his thoughtless questions. He'd dislodged the cap on his memories, made Daniel recall things in his nightmares that he didn't want to think about in the light of day.

As to following Corey's story in the press, yes, he'd done that. The investigation into the crashed plane was officially closed. That was something he did know.

Evidence was conclusive. The engine had suffered a bird strike. Somehow the plane had gone into a steep dive, and the children left behind had lost their parents and uncle in an unforeseen tragedy. The papers reported the information dryly, but at least one of them had been sly in reminding their readers that the pilot, Corey's father, had been thought to have possibly crashed the plane deliberately into the mountain, in a horrific act of murder-suicide. Killing himself, his wife, and his brother. Of course, they withdrew the article, but even though that ugly concept had gotten shut down, surely the mud would stick. Other stories had explained that Corey's father had been a good man. A family man who loved his kids and his wife. Not one said much about Drake other than that he was a businessman.

In the end, it appeared that the crash had really been nothing more than a tragic accident, and Daniel hoped the conclusion brought Corey some peace.

Also, weirdly, Daniel felt like he owed Corey something.

For the longest time, he'd waited, always on edge, to be called up to give evidence as to what kind of man Drake Dryden had been. He'd expected Corey to involve the cops, but somehow his assurance that he didn't want to do that had been the truth. There had been no contact with the police or even from a PI like the one Corey's dad had hired.

Even though his reaction to the man's voice on the video had been primal, the sound itself had never found its way into Daniel's nightmares. And there was never any mention of evidence given over by the family in support of their father, so they must have decided not to make the journals, or Daniel's possible evidence, public.

So yeah, he owed Corey for that.

Corey was on his mind a lot. They shared something hateful through his uncle. A vicious, sickening, soul-destroying connection. But quite apart from all that, Daniel remembered the compassion and sorrow in Corey's eyes, along with the fear for his sisters, and anger, and a familiar mess of emotions that Daniel could empathize with. Corey's life had become something else when that plane crashed, and one day, Daniel thought maybe he'd look the man up and see if they could talk rationally without temper and resentment and accusation.

They'd held hands briefly, and he recalled the warmth

of Corey's touch and the unshed tears in his eyes. Then the devil on his shoulder took his nice feelings away.

*He doesn't know me. I'm just another victim. A reminder.*

Daniel closed his eyes and tilted his head back to breathe in the fresh air from the second skylight, forcing himself not to think about Corey or what he might learn from him.

Corey was the kind of man that Daniel could be attracted to. He wanted a man one day, a man who knew things about him that he didn't have to explain. One with a strong heart.

That was why he was alone. Because no one had a heart big enough, or strong enough, for Daniel to trust them.

Maybe after today, he would look up Corey again, see how he was doing.

Then, wrapped in a towel, he moved back to the main room and made up the bed. He might not be staying for long, but it would be at least one night, so he ticked bed-making off his list.

Next, he dressed in clean clothes and shoved his bags under the bed, checking they were well back. In the lighter bag were most of his worldly goods, enough clothes for three days, underwear, T-shirts, jeans, a sweater, and a thin jacket. In the other were his books, six hardbacks he didn't go anywhere without. Someone had once told him that they were all available on Kindle, but Kindles meant a connection to an electronic world, and he hated that thought as much as he hated the concept of owning a phone. Finally, with nothing else to do, he moved the chair from the door and unlocked it, stepping out into the waning sunshine, wondering what the hell to do next.

And he walked right into the man he'd tried so hard to forget, the one with the strong heart and strong family morals, who had held his hand and cried for him.

Corey Dryden.

## Chapter Eight

COREY STOPPED, UNSURE IF HE WAS HALLUCINATING, AND Sophie barreled into him making him stumble forward. He caught himself, and her, in time so they didn't both end up on the ground, and she giggled as he swung her up to his shoulders. She was getting almost too big for him to do that, but according to her, lifts and carries stopped when she got to her next birthday. Not yet.

She'd been clingy ever since the report on the crash had been made public a few weeks back. Knowing that the crash had been a terrible accident didn't make the incident any easier to take for him or for his sisters.

Sophie had woken up at least four times this month crying and ended up sleeping with him on the sofa watching a kid's movie *over and over again*. He didn't know what he'd wanted the report to come back with. Finding out that his dad had deliberately crashed the plane wouldn't have been of any use to anyone. There would have been no closure, and old wounds would have been exposed even more. A bird strike was real and unfortunate, and a horrific end to the flight.

Sophie couldn't understand how the birds in the air could have killed their parents and uncle, and Corey had no idea how to make her understand. He'd found her this morning, emptying the bird feeders of all their seeds and nuts, holding an umbrella over her head in case a bird flew at her.

And now she'd sat next to him in the car, and he'd made her laugh, but there had still been confusion and sadness in her eyes. Coming to Legacy Ranch was good for her.

"Gotcha," she squealed, right in his ear, and he winced before helping her back to the ground. She hadn't seen *him*, standing in the sunlight, and was tugging on Corey's hand, demanding a drink. That was what they'd come back to the house for after spending an hour digging through the earth and planting flowers.

"You go on in, Spud. Jason said he was making lemonade."

"Will there be birds here today?"

Corey could say no, but he'd determined she didn't want him to lie. She needed truth.

"Maybe, but they stay way up, and they don't hurt us."

"M'okay."

"Hey, Sophie!" Amelia called her over from just inside the kitchen door. She was staying in pod seven, a slim, small girl, who missed her sister after her family threw her out when she got pregnant. She'd taken a shine to Sophie, and hell, Corey was pleased to see someone else could make Sophie smile. She looked as if she was close to having the baby now and wondered how the dynamic between her and Sophie would change. He hoped not too much.

She darted away, glanced at *him* as she ran past, and grinned wide before vanishing through the main door.

"Daniel?" Corey finally asked, needing to know he hadn't actually spent too much time in the sun. Even though Sophie had seen a man there and grinned at him, he wasn't sure it was really the man he couldn't get out of his head.

The one he'd asked so many questions. The one he felt all the guilt about.

"Corey." Daniel sounded wary as if he wasn't sure what reception he would get.

He stared at Daniel, dumbly. Then, as if manners suddenly switched on, he moved closer and extended a hand to him.

"You're looking well," he lied.

Actually, Daniel appeared exhausted, thinner than he remembered, and way too pale. Kyle had never given up on Daniel one day coming to Legacy, but whatever had driven him to come here had to be eating away at him. Corey had an image in his head of what Daniel had looked like. Tall, blond, with dark eyes and a serious expression, was how Corey had cataloged the man who'd lost so much, and he'd thought of him often.

"You didn't tell anyone? About what I said," Daniel blurted out and then crossed his arms over his chest and tipped his chin up. It didn't make him seem any more confident. In fact, he appeared vulnerable and was obviously faking it.

"The inquest said the crash was an accident. That is all I wanted for my family. For a reason to exist that meant my parents didn't leave us intentionally. Something for my sisters to live with. There's no point in exposing the rest."

Daniel scuffed one toe in the dirt. "Okay." Then neither of them knew what to do or say next. At least, Corey didn't, and Daniel was just quiet.

"I need to go...my sister..." Corey said and then spun on his heel and followed Sophie into the kitchen. There was actually no sign of Jason. Instead, Liam was at the table, and he found Sophie chatting away to him as Liam mixed batter in a bowl and listened to Sophie talk about a TV show she loved.

"Corey, can we pick the carrots yet?" She launched into the questions as soon as he stepped inside, not skipping a beat between talking about an animated teddy bear to focusing on Corey. "Liam says we have to wait, but he doesn't know all the things you and Jason do."

Corey smiled at his sister, going into autopilot and focusing on her and not on the fact that Daniel was here at Legacy.

"I think even Liam knows way more than I do." In the last few months, Sophie had taken to following Corey everywhere. To her, there was nothing he didn't do the best, or fastest, but at the same time as his relationship with his other two sisters was strained. "Is Kyle here?"

Kyle was never in one place long. Either out with the horses, or in his office, or working on construction, or at anything he could find that would keep him busy. Corey knew though that Saturday was office day, and there was a vague chance of pinning him down.

"He just went in." Liam inclined his head to the office door.

"Where's Jason?" Unspoken was the question as to

why Liam was here on a Saturday, and there was no sign of Jason. "Is everything okay?"

"Jason is up at the D. I came down to visit with Daniel."

There, the elephant in the room. Corey took a seat. "I can't believe he's here."

Liam stared at him for the longest time, thoughtfully. "You and me both, but I'm glad for it."

"Yeah."

"How are you doing with seeing him?"

"I wasn't expecting to see him, but I have a lot I want to say to him, to say sorry." There were no secrets there. The first day he'd come to Legacy, he'd told Kyle outright what he knew, but Kyle had taken it as if the information didn't matter, told him that he'd closed that box, and hoped it would stay shut. Liam and Gabriel had pretty much said the same thing, even as much as Corey wanted to apologize for any part his uncle had played in what had happened.

Liam looked at the door as if he expected Daniel to come in right there and then. "He doesn't need to hear you say sorry, dude. It's not your fault, and the only sorry we would ever want are from the ones who..."

*Hurt us.*

He didn't finish, inclining his head to Sophie who was concentrating on separating M&Ms into piles.

"Yeah, I know. Doesn't make me want to say it any less."

"My advice? For what it's worth?"

"Please."

"Stop with the sorry and start with the normal parts of

life. Hello, and how are you, and what are you up to. That kind of thing."

Corey pressed a kiss to Sophie's head. "I'll be back in a bit, Spud. Help Liam."

"M'okay," she said, and the last he saw was her demanding the spoon to help Liam stir and to add in the M&Ms she'd so carefully sorted. What he was making, Corey couldn't tell, but there were chocolate chips in a bowl, along with the M&Ms, and he hoped the thin batter was for pancakes or something as good. Jason had a way with food and found as much peace in that as Kyle did with his horses and as much as Corey did with the kitchen garden, but he'd never seen Liam cook before. In fact, Liam didn't spend weekends at Legacy. He was busy having a love life and working at the D.

Every weekend Corey stayed at Legacy, craving a quiet calm in contrast to his week, which was meetings and paperwork at a shitty, messy prison of a company. Sophie would come with him and throw herself into ranch life as if she'd been born into it. If only he could get Amy and Chloe to visit, then they could spend quality time here as a family away from the house and the memories of the people who'd lived there. He was sure of it.

The garden at the back of the Legacy Ranch was something that'd been started a while back, but no one had wanted to take care of it. Corey had spent so much time when he was younger working with his mom in her rose garden, mulching and pruning and helping her dig into the dark earth. Just the scent of the yard they were working on brought memories of her back to him. It was irrigated with gray water from the ranch, full of vegetables, and even a few roses at the front that seemed to be thriving. His mom said there was value in growing your own vegetables, of being organic, and her spirit lived on in this garden. Or so he liked to think.

He knocked on the door and pushed it open at the "come in" from inside. Kyle wasn't at his desk. He was standing by the window staring out at the land beyond, the horses grazing there.

"Hey." He didn't move from the window. Corey shut the door behind him, and Kyle raised an eyebrow in question.

"I saw Daniel," Corey murmured.

"Robbie met him walking in. Two bags. Looks tired."

"How long is he staying?"

"I don't know."

"Did he say why he was here?"

"He's entitled to privacy as much as any other person who comes here. Corey, you know that I can't tell—"

"Oh jeez, no, I don't want to ask questions like that. I'm just... Liam says I should stop with saying sorry, but, Kyle, please, what do I say to him?"

Kyle turned from the window, his expression guarded. "About what, exactly?"

His tone wasn't hurtful, but the implication was there in his simple question. Legacy had become an oasis of peace for Corey and Sophie, and the same would be available to any person who ended up here. No one here asked questions. They quietly listened to anyone who wanted to share their pain or their thoughts.

Frustration shot through Corey. "I wish I'd known he was going to be here. Then I could have said something constructive when I saw him instead of nothing at all. I could have given him an apology that counted, not a normal sorry, but a real try at forgiveness for what Drake did. I could have made him see that I understood what he'd gone through. Talked to him about compensation, begun to make it right, face-to-face. Because compensation isn't sorry, is it? It could make a difference, help him to cover his new life."

Kyle sighed deeply and then leaned on the window sill. "Corey, you need to breathe, calm down, and think about what you're saying."

Corey stared at Kyle, who didn't look away, and he felt numb to everything. Grief snuck up on him in such a vile way, a stealthy twist of pain that he'd kept ignoring for months until now it was crashing over him. Consuming him.

Just like the first day he'd arrived at the D, Sophie next to him, and the floodgates had opened.

He still recalled the day vividly. Riley taking Sophie to see the horses and leaving him to talk to Jack. Somehow they'd gone from Corey not knowing which way to turn, to agreeing to try working at Legacy, on a new kitchen garden, the next weekend, to bring Sophie, and to help Legacy work on their yard. He'd been there ten weekends since then. The hours in the garden were therapeutic, and he'd had time to think and bond with his youngest sister, who loved everything about Legacy.

Of course, he had to go home Sunday evening; he had a business to run, a house to watch over, sisters to take care of, and misery to dwell in.

Kyle still stared at him, and Corey closed his eyes. No, he didn't know what Daniel had gone through. No, Daniel didn't want anything to do with the estate. No, there was nothing he could say that would make things right for

Daniel.

"What brings people here is nothing to do with me, or you, or Jack and Riley. Are you going to be cool with Daniel, not make yourself feel better by pushing him into a corner? Give him his space?"

Corey nodded. He knew that was what he should do.

He wanted to ask Kyle more, but the office phone rang, and Kyle answered immediately.

"Gabe," he murmured, "hang on." He covered the receiver. "I need to take this," he apologized.

Corey backed out of the room and closed the door. He assumed Gabriel would be visiting now, seeing Daniel for himself. Maybe even helping him. It was no surprise to see Liam still sitting at the table with Sophie.

With Gabriel visiting as well, the four boys would be together.

Liam, Kyle, Gabriel, Daniel; they would have a lot to talk about.

"Hey Spud, how about we go now—"

"No, Corey, I don't wanna go."

Corey held up a hand to stop her arguing and thank god she was still young enough to listen to him.

"We can go by the horses, then get takeout on the way home and spend the evening with Amy and Chloe."

"They won't be home," Sophie finally said, biting her lower lip. "They never are."

She was right, Amy was out more than she was in, spending time with her boyfriend, and as for Chloe. She'd begun to stay out longer and longer with friends or spend time in her room. Corey was losing control of everything and everyone, and he saw his family fracturing in front of him.

"What if we go find them both then? We could all sit in the office."

Her eyes widened. They hadn't sat in there as a family in months, and it was the only real connection they had to their parents.

"Can we? For real?"

Corey was aware that Liam was watching this play out with undisguised curiosity, but now wasn't the time to stand around explaining their history and how he was fucking everything up. Now was the time to leave before Daniel had to be in any kind of position where he had to talk to Corey.

*I must remind him of what Drake did to him. How can he bear to see me?*

Maybe they wouldn't be able to come back at all. If this was Daniel's sanctuary, then there wasn't a place here for him and Sophie. The thought of leaving the garden and throwing away the connection he'd worked so hard on with his little sister made his heart hurt.

"Of course we can. Let's go."

Sophie scrambled down, grabbing a last cookie, and Corey opened his mouth to tell her not to eat too many, but he wasn't Mom, and what right did he have to say a single fucking thing?

They'd almost made it to the door when it opened and the one person he'd hoped to avoid walked in.

"Hey," Corey murmured.

"Hi," Daniel said. As soon as he could, he helped Sophie out and hustled her to the car.

Daniel followed them, and suddenly it was him and Daniel standing alone.

"I think maybe we should talk?" Daniel began, pushing his hands into his jean pockets, his shoulders lifting.

"What about?" Corey could feel his stomach twisting, not knowing what Daniel might want to say to him. Or hell, what Corey might find himself saying back. Thinking about Daniel as something other than the boy his uncle hurt was opening a whole new can of worms. He was pale, yes, and skinny, yes, but there was a strength in Daniel that Corey was drawn to. Not to mention his soft smile as he stood there, evidently thinking just as hard about what to say as Corey was.

"I don't know. I'm not good at this shit."

"Neither am I at the moment," Corey said. Part of him had hoped that maybe he and Daniel could find common ground to shoot the breeze. Perhaps even strike up a loose friendship.

"Corey!" Sophie called.

*Saved by the bell, or the shouting sister, or whatever.*

"I have to go."

"I know."

Corey backed away, the car only a few steps behind him, belted in and drove away, checking in his mirror to see the lone shadowy figure watching him leave. Sophie chattered incessantly about gardening and horses and how Mom used to make better cookies, and Corey let it wash over him as they made their way home.

All he could think of was that Daniel deserved to find a place to stay and that Corey didn't really need Legacy at all.

*I just won't go back. Simple.*

There was no sign of Amy when they got home. Only a note on the massive fridge in their expansive kitchen explaining she was out with Michael.

The boy seemed friendly enough. Not that he was a *boy* at all. He was actually only a few years younger than Corey and carving a career in a real estate office. He drove a car, had an apartment over his parent's garage, and Amy was twenty-two so he couldn't stop her from going out and enjoying her life. He didn't want to do that at all.

Chloe, on the other hand, was sprawled on the sofa in the TV room, a bag of chips in her lap and a can of Coke on its side on the rug, the brown liquid splashed and staining the cream. Mom would have had a fit seeing that. She'd have found the small carpet steamer, cleaned the mess, and made Chloe see that Coke was a *horrible thing*. All Corey could do was pick up the can and stare at his sleeping sister.

Her long curly hair was ebony this week, with two streaks of white, and her face was plastered with thick makeup. She wasn't the Chloe that she'd been, but the family counselor talked about grief manifesting in all kinds of ways and that Corey should back off.

Okay, so she didn't use those words but giving Chloe her space was something he needed to do, apparently.

He wanted to ride roughshod over her and tell her to talk to him, but obviously, an expert in grief counseling was a better person than he was.

"Amy isn't here," Sophie called loudly from the stairs, causing Chloe to stir and open her eyes. Of course, it had to happen the moment Corey was staring at her, contemplating life.

"What the hell, Corey!" she screeched at the top of her

voice, rolling upright, her hair pressed flat on one side of her head.

Corey flailed for something to say. "You spilled your drink," he finally managed, and she looked from him to the Coke.

"So?"

"So, it stains the carpet."

She sneered. "Then we'll get a cleaner in. We have the money." She pouted, and then shoved past him. "Freak," she muttered as she swept past.

Corey's last nerve snapped.

"Chloe Elizabeth Dryden, come back here!"

She stopped dead and pivoted on her feet, her expression unreadable. "What?"

*Stay here and talk. Be with your sister. Be my sister.*

But the words escaped him when he realized he didn't have the energy to start anything with anyone today. "Nothing."

She shook her head. "That's what I thought. Jesus, Corey."

When she ran up the stairs, Sophie stepped into the room, and there were real tears in her eyes. He opened up his arms for her to come in for a hug, but she didn't move; she just cried.

"I hate everything," she said when he stepped toward her. Then she too went up the stairs as fast as her little legs could take her.

Leaving Corey in the middle of the front room, his head hurting, and his heart ragged with the fear of the cracks in his family. He could blame teenage angst for Chloe, a new boyfriend for Amy, even being too young to understand for Sophie, but at the core of it, he was scared to see the cracks in his family now he was in charge.

*Mom, Dad, I wish you were here.*

## Chapter Nine

"COREY'S HERE EVERY WEEKEND," LIAM SAID BEFORE Daniel opened his mouth.

It had taken him a good ten minutes of standing outside the door before he pushed his way inside, and that effort had stolen his ability to care about why Corey was here. "Sophie is his little sister, and she loves the horses and the garden."

"I didn't ask," Daniel snapped and stood uneasily by the closed door.

"Okay, then," Liam said as if Daniel hadn't just been abrupt and rude.

Daniel felt the guilt rise inside him. Liam didn't deserve him being an idiot who couldn't even manage basic manners. "Sorry."

Liam grinned at him and shrugged. "No biggie. Coffee?"

"Water. I'll get it." Daniel took an offered glass and filled it with water from the tap. No one would have messed with water that everyone drank. Right?

"Cookie? I made chocolate chip, peanut butter, caramel."

Familiar anxiety gripped him at choices in food he hadn't seen prepared.

*If you can't trust Liam, then who can you trust?*

"I'm not hungry."

Liam nodded but left the plate of cookies out anyway. Daniel knew that in a few minutes he'd be able to make a decision, but not even the lure of chocolate made him want to eat right now. Seeing Corey confused him. He'd tried not to think about him, and what he'd found him to say. For a long time, Daniel even blamed Corey for not being able to settle in work, to be so damn fucked in the head. But it wasn't Corey. It was his own mess, and he needed to own it.

"You must want a cookie?" Liam asked again and pushed the plate toward Daniel.

Because Liam was so determined, Daniel cautiously took one that was filled to bursting with chocolate and placed it on the table in front of him. At least that would stop Liam from asking.

"What is Corey doing here?" The question needed to be asked because it was all he could think about. It was even more important than beginning to understand why he'd decided to get his ass out here.

"Jack suggested it." Liam shrugged. "He was struggling with his sisters. Usual thing I guess."

There was nothing *usual* about Corey, but Daniel bit his tongue. An internal door opened, startling Daniel, and he stood, the chair he'd been sitting on falling over. *Jesus, what is it with my inability to keep a chair upright for fuck's sake*. He relaxed a little when he realized it was only Kyle.

"I called Gabriel to come visit us." He took a seat and helped himself to two cookies and some black coffee.

"Uh-huh," Liam offered as if this wasn't a huge thing. The three of them sat around a table eating cookies and drinking coffee as if nothing had happened to each of them. Words were trapped in Daniel's head. Vicious, acidic thoughts that ate away at him. How could Kyle and Liam sit there so calmly, so utterly at peace? Did they not feel as if they had snakes in their bellies? Daniel snapped the cookie he'd chosen in half, then quarters, then even smaller, picking out all the chocolate in it, and his world was unfocused, a blur of chocolate and crumbs, and still, he couldn't vocalize any of it. When he couldn't see a thing, when his eyes were so full of tears, and the grief bubbled out of him, he pushed aside the crumbs, scraped them on the floor in angry swipes, rested his head on his arms, and cried.

He felt someone touch his shoulder, shrugged off the sensation of it, and ignored the gentle words of encouragement. He heard doors open, and words, and sounds, and knew he should lift his head, but it was too heavy. Finally, when the pain that banded his skull was less anguish and more an ache from his crying, he shifted in his seat a little. Fuck knew how long he'd cried for the injustice and the terror and the pain that burned in him. An hour? More?

Scrubbing at his eyes and wiping his nose on his, shirt he attempted to sit up, but lightheaded, he began to slip sideways on the chair. Arms caught him, and he clung for his life to whoever held him.

*Stupid, pathetic, crying won't fix anything.*

Another door opened and closed, and he blinked at the gust of cooler air that fanned over his face, blinking at a figure in the doorway. One from the dreams he had of the day he'd found the courage to face his abusers in court. Gabriel.

The figure crossed to him immediately. Pulled him in for a hug that he couldn't have stopped if he'd tried, and with wet eyes and a runny nose and words that just wouldn't come, he cried that last little bit against a beautiful, soft suit and breathed in the scent of something comforting.

"Everything is gonna be okay," Gabriel murmured. "We'll get through this together."

Shame flooded him, and then curiously it vanished, and in its place, he felt the warmth of hope.

---

The cookies were gone, and, in their stead, Liam and Kyle had created a whole table of food to pick at, from chips and dips to pieces of hot barbecue chicken and a massive bowl of coleslaw. Daniel took some painkillers when they were offered, and the glass of water that came with it. He realized, with some trepidation, that he trusted the three men here. After all, they were the same.

"So you have a degree," Gabriel commented, wiping his face free of barbecue sauce with a paper towel. There were no fancy napkins here at all, and no one stood on ceremony. He'd even witnessed Liam and Gabriel good-naturedly fighting over the last piece of chicken. A battle that Liam won because he'd distracted Gabriel by making him look out of the window. They were like kids, and it felt good. He pulled himself back to thinking about the comment on his education.

"Yeah."

"What in?"

*Nothing worth talking about. Not something useful like chemistry or math. Stop it.*

"Marketing, business. That sort of thing."

Gabriel steepled his fingers and rested his chin on them. "I never got even the minimum at school, couldn't hack it."

"Me neither," Kyle agreed, and Liam nodded.

Gabriel huffed. "Although I'd maybe want to try to do something, you know, because Cameron is the kind of man who debates all sorts of things, and I sometimes feel…" He shrugged. He didn't need to finish.

"As if you can't keep up." Kyle sighed. "I have that sometimes. When I have a black day, and I don't understand why I'm feeling so bad, that is the day that Jason will come up with some complicated theory about aliens or something, and I don't follow half of what he says."

"Marcus wanted to debate brown and white bread. I just gave him my look. Or at least the look he describes as mine. Apparently, it's halfway between constipation and disbelief." Liam snorted a laugh at his words.

"Are these your…?" Was boyfriends the right word to use? Were the three of them even in a place to have someone meaningful in their lives?

The others exchanged quick glances, nothing awful, only checking what they should be saying, he guessed.

"Marcus is my partner," Liam began. "He has a

company working with surrogates. I met him when he helped Jack and Riley start a family. He had a hard time getting to know me. I chased him away too many times to remember. Guess he wanted me enough to stay focused on what he desired." Liam smiled.

Everything was quiet, then Gabriel cleared his throat. "Cameron is my guy. He owns a hotel in the city. I was selling myself, and he hired me as his date, then rescued me from an abusive relationship, before we channeled *Pretty Woman* and I rescued him right back." He grinned.

Daniel waited for Gabriel's voice to crack, but it didn't. Somehow, he'd come to terms with what he'd done and the decisions he'd made in his life. Sometimes, when money was short, he'd considered that sex had been something forced on him, and actually, he should go out there and get paid for it. He didn't because every time he got close to the breadline, more funding would come in from his scholarship.

"Then there's my man," Kyle said. "You've not met Jason yet, but he'll be back tomorrow. He's spending the night up with Robbie and Eli, to give us some space. He's…" He shook his head. "I don't know how to describe him. He's a live-wire, an uncontainable mischief-maker, who's constantly in everyone's space, and who keeps me sane."

"You've all been lucky," Daniel murmured. He wanted to add that he couldn't wait to meet the other men because that was polite, but even the idea of meeting Jason, the most likely given he lived there, made his insides churn again.

They talked about ranching, horses, the weather, Jack, and Riley, about life in general, and it was midnight before everything finally caught up with Daniel because he'd been running on fumes. When the small group parted, Liam up to the other ranch, Gabriel in his car, and Kyle to the sink to clear up, Daniel could have left and gone back to his room.

He knew he needed sleep and all the windows and doors locked in that room, but then he would wake up, and have a hundred uncertainties in his head. He hovered by the door as if he were a child waiting to be dismissed and hating that he even felt that way.

"Kyle?"

"Uh-huh?"

"If you need my room for someone else tonight, y'know, like a kid who turns up and needs help, tell me, and I can get a cab out of here."

Kyle turned from the sink and leaned on the counter.

"That place is yours."

Daniel blinked at him. "For tonight, yeah, I know, but it's okay."

Kyle straightened and wiped his hands on a dishcloth. "Let me show you something in my office." He went through the other door, but Daniel didn't move from his spot. He waited until Kyle came back out with a tube. He pulled out rolled-up papers, then laid them out, each top corner held down with a salt-and-pepper shaker respectively, a mug on the bottom left, and the other corner under his hand.

"Look at this." He pointed at what looked like a set of plans. Daniel edged toward the table and peered at whatever Kyle had his index finger on. The writing was small, and he had to lean quite close, but there in block lettering were two words. *Daniel's room*. Next to it was *Gabriel's room*.

"What is that?"

"When we built Legacy, it was vital to Jack that we have a space for the two of you if you ever needed it. He added it as extra, made the rooms bigger, a home if you needed one. Of course, Gabriel never uses his now, and he and Cameron sponsor any kids who need that space."

"Jack built me a home? Why didn't he tell me?"

Kyle lifted his hand, and the plan curled up a little. "That's not him. He just had one thing in mind when he began to create Legacy with Darren Castille. To give safety to any kid who needed it, but that doesn't stop when someone turns eighteen. Jason was older than that when he came here, by a long way. So you see, you're welcome to stay here as long as you want."

"And help out. That is what Jack said."

Kyle smiled then, and the smile reached his eyes. "We have so much we need to work on, outreach, computer skills for some of the kids who come here, the website, working with Darren and Steve. I don't think you've met Steve, right? He's married to Riley's sister, and he works at a center in the city, and Darren, you remember him, yeah?"

Daniel nodded, which was about as much as he could do when someone with the Castille name was mentioned.

"He'll probably come back with Jason tomorrow, but you don't have to meet up with him or with Jason. You don't have to do anything you don't want to do. Although with Jason not here, we could do with some help mucking out the stalls in the morning."

The thought of doing something, *anything*, was exactly

what he needed. Repetitive work that he could be good at again was bigger than the worry about what he'd be in the barns.

"I can try," he said.

"Good enough. You want to take some food to your room?"

Daniel didn't have a chance to answer when Kyle thrust a container of cookies at him and a brand-new unopened bottle of water, along with a to-go cup of hot chocolate. Daniel juggled the whole lot carefully and turned to leave, Kyle opening the door for him. Daniel almost made it away without having to talk any more.

"Daniel?"

He turned to face Kyle. "Yeah?"

"It's really good to have you here."

"It feels right to be here," Daniel replied then headed for his new home for the night. It didn't matter if he stayed one day or more, Kyle had said he had a place here.

That meant more than anyone would ever know.

He opened the skylights, just enough to get air and not let in the rain if the skies decided to dump the wet stuff on this part of Texas. Then he stored the cookies in a cupboard, drank the hot chocolate, and pushed the water to the back of the desk. Finally, he lay back on his bed.

He wasn't feeling safe. It might be a while before he felt really safe anywhere, but he was settled right at this moment. Sleep didn't come easy, and he decided quickly that the crying may have dislodged a few too many of those hidden fears. Then there was seeing Corey and wondering what it might be like to hug a man like him or hold his hand. He imagined he would never be able to sleep.

But the bed was comfortable, the sky was dark, the stars bright, and he was sheltered there.

That was good enough, and he slept.

The dream started the same as it always did. He was in pain, but soft hands stopped that pain, long hair slid over his face, and whoever held him told him that she was sorry and that everything would be okay. He thought maybe it was an angel.

He'd become conditioned to waking up when the dream changed into a nightmare.

It was safer that way.

## Chapter Ten

COREY WOKE ABRUPTLY AND FOUGHT THE SHEET TO GET out of bed, unsure of why he'd so dramatically yanked himself from his dreams. Particularly on a Saturday, when he had no reason to get up too early. Not since he'd stopped going to Legacy. Okay, so it had only been two weeks, but he was determined that not going was absolutely the best decision to make. Of course, Sophie hated it, and last weekend he'd felt so sorry that he'd dug up half of his mom's rose garden to create a vegetable bed. Not that this made any difference. Sophie still wasn't talking to him, and Amy had screamed at him for destroying that important part of their mother.

What could he do? He had to give Daniel his space, and he didn't know any other way of making things right.

*Everyone wants* me *to be the one to make things right.*

Tired and yawning, bleary-eyed and needing coffee, Corey found broken glass on the kitchen floor in the worst possible way. Cursing at the immediate pain that knifed through him, he stumbled backward and hopped to the light switch, wondering what the fuck he'd just walked on.

The remains of crystal wine glassed was scattered in a carpet of pain to the fridge, milk in puddles with the containers on their sides, jars of jelly smashed against the wall, and worst of all, the coffee machine on its side in a mess of sticky syrup.

Fear struck him that someone had broken into the house and he needed to call the cops. His second thought was that his foot hurt like a fucker, and then his rational brain kicked in, and he processed what the priorities were. He grabbed a tea towel and sat on the nearest chair, pulling out the shard of glass that had impaled him and wiping at the blood. The cut wasn't too bad. The shape of the shard enough so that it was shallow and long as opposed to deep and dangerous. Still, the damn thing kept bleeding, so he twisted the towel around his foot and held it there as he surveyed the damage. Now he needed to deal with potential intruders.

"What the fuck?"

He'd left his cell in his room, and the nearest landline phone was on the other side of the kitchen.

*Two minutes and then hopefully the bleeding will stop, and I can call the cops.*

Then he heard the noise and stiffened. It sounded like a whimper. He reached for the nearest thing he could grab, which turned out to be a shattered wine bottle, the contents on the floor mixing in with milk and curdling into a mess that turned his stomach.

Cautiously, he rounded the cupboards, watching out for stray glass, then carefully placed the remains of the bottle on the counter.

Chloe was curled into a ball in the corner of the breakfast nook, her head in her hands, and the sound he'd heard was her crying.

She didn't seem hurt, not a victim of some random break-in, and he instinctively knew it had been her who had caused the destruction.

"Chloe?"

She lifted her face, her eyes red and swollen, her face pale, and her long hair had been cut off and lay around her in a pile as dramatic as the glass. The grief was there in his sister, and he slid onto the bench next to her. He didn't say anything, but he took one of her hands and held it tight.

"It's okay," he murmured.

"It's really not," she said in reply but didn't yank her hand away. Instead, she leaned on him.

"What did you do to your hair?"

She shrugged and then sighed. "Mom's hair was always so beautiful. She didn't dye it, or curl it, or straighten it. She just left it, and it was gorgeous."

Corey made a soft noise of agreement, traversing that weird landmine-strewn land of female reasoning when it came to hair and makeup.

"So I cut off all the stuff that was black, all the destroyed mess, and thought it would fix how I felt, but it didn't, and then I accidentally dropped the peanut butter, and the noise it made on the tile was so good. So I threw the wine glasses, the jelly, and the wine, and then the milk, and it made me feel better. Until it didn't."

"I get it," Corey added with a rueful laugh.

"I'll be eighteen in a month."

"I know," Corey lied. Abstractly, he knew his middle sister was turning eighteen soon, but in the mess of everything he'd had to think about, he hadn't realized it was so close.

"You do?" she asked.

"Absolutely. We have all kinds of things planned."

*I'm so good at this lying thing.*

That made Chloe snort out loud. "You so forgot, and it's okay, but now you know…"

"Party, right, got it."

"No, I don't want anything like that. Just us four, pizza and a movie. Actually, if Amy wants her boyfriend here, he can come, but only because I said so."

"Okay."

"And you can bring a boyfriend if you want to. Do you have one?"

Corey shook his head. "Not right now." The only thing close to affection was a curling need inside him to hold Daniel, and that had to be just a sympathy thing. "Maybe I'll go hunt one down soon."

"Could I bring a special friend?"

"Of course you can."

"What if that person was my *girlfriend*?"

He didn't see anything wrong with that, and then the emphasis she'd used hit him. "Not a friend who is a girl, but a *girl*friend."

"Yes."

He hugged her. "I think that would be wonderful." It made him so happy that she'd come out to him in a few short sentences. His own coming out had been pretty much the same with his parents. A few words, acceptance, some limited questions, and then everything had been okay. He could feel his parents there in that moment, guiding his hand, and tears threatened. But Chloe hadn't finished.

"Also, I think maybe I'd like to go to that farm place where you go to with Sophie and see what's going on there. She loves it, and it's made her too sad not to go. We should go. All of us. Today."

Corey bit back the need to tell her they couldn't go there anymore, and instead, he thought about the benefits to Sophie and maybe to Chloe. He lifted an arm to pull her in for a hug.

"Deal."

They sat in silence, for the longest time. Then Chloe cursed. "You're bleeding."

He chuckled. The throb of pain had eased, and the bleeding had stopped now, even if the tea towel was dramatically scarlet.

"That's what comes from standing on glass."

Chloe snuggled into him. "My bad."

---

Sophie couldn't sit still in the back of the car, wriggling, and bouncing and telling Corey about all she wanted to do when they got to Legacy. He'd sent Chloe upstairs, cleared up the mess in the kitchen, all before six in the morning. Now they were parked outside a salon, one that opened at eight, and Chloe was inside having something done with her hair.

Girl's stuff.

"Where is she!" Sophie demanded, for what must have been the twentieth time she asked.

"She'll be out in a minute," Corey replied as he had done every time.

And thank god, he wasn't lying, because the door

opened, and Chloe headed to the car. She opened the passenger door and belted up, then turned to look at Corey with an expectant expression.

"So?" she asked and reached up to touch her hair, which had been cut short and feathered around her face.

Corey's breath caught in his throat. "You look so much like Mom," he whispered.

She smiled, even though she had tears in her eyes. "Thank you."

He started the car and pulled away from the salon, heading south. *One more stop.*

The house they parked outside was nothing fancy, certainly not as big as their house, but everything about the place promised friendly and welcoming. He knocked on the front door, and a man carrying a newspaper opened it.

"Can I help?" he asked, pushing glasses up his nose and half-smiling. Evidently, he was one of those people who didn't immediately assume the worst when someone they didn't know turned up on their doorstep.

"I'm here for my sister," Corey said. "I'm Corey Dryden. Can I talk to her?"

"Adrian Thompson," the man said, and they shook hands. "Of course, come in, they've just come in from the apartment and are up in the spare room looking at old photos."

Corey glanced back at his sisters in the car and then stepped in.

"Michael, Amy, come down here a minute."

He heard the sound of steps on the stairs and an unfamiliar sound. One he hadn't heard in a while. Amy laughing.

Of course, that stopped when she reached the bottom

of the stairs and saw him standing there. If anything, she was scared.

"Oh my god, what's happened? Is it Sophie? Chloe?" She clung to her boyfriend.

Guilt punched Corey in the gut. "Nothing, *shit*, nothing. The girls are fine, I promise. I just wanted to ask you to come to Legacy Ranch with us today."

"Why?" she asked suspiciously. "You never asked before."

"I did." It hit him that perhaps he hadn't explicitly asked her, aware she had her boyfriend and that she'd been the strongest of them through all of this. That maybe he considered she didn't *need* somewhere like Legacy. But the siblings couldn't entirely heal if they were apart.

"No, you haven't asked me."

He shook his head, "I guess I didn't. But Sophie is heartbroken I stopped going, and Chloe had a…" He paused, looked at the father and son, who watched him with interest. "…a thing," he finished.

"I'd love to," Amy said, then leaned up to kiss her boyfriend on the cheek, Michael smiling and hugging her.

"Have fun," he offered and tweaked her nose.

When they were outside, Amy spoke under her breath. "What was Chloe's *thing*? Is she okay?"

And all Corey could say was, "She will be."

He listened to his sisters talk about hairstyles and makeup and heard Amy tell Chloe how gorgeous her pixie cut was. The sun was shining when they turned off the road and headed onto Double D land, taking the turnoff for Legacy.

Sophie was out as soon as the engine stopped, running toward the cabin, but Chloe and Amy didn't move so fast.

"What do we do now?" Amy asked, twisting in her seat, so she faced Corey. He had to tell them the truth. Someday it would come out, and lies were the worst thing to keep. The PI hadn't found anything else, The case was done as far as everyone involved. At least it was done for Corey and his family. The bird strike in the crash investigation was enough for suspicious fingers to stop pointing at Corey's dad, but the damage had been done. The board was worried, and at first, Corey had been pissed, but then over the last few weeks, he'd become less anxious and more focused on his family.

Which led to the next thing he had to talk to his sisters about.

"Can we have a quick talk?" He indicated for Chloe to take out her earbuds. "We've all had offers on our percentage holdings of Dryden-Marsdale, and I'm inclined to say we accept it."

"But that's Dad's company," Chloe said. "What would we do without it?"

Corey thought about where to start this. "I would make enough money on the sale of my part to enable us to not worry about things for some time, to get you and Sophie through college, and I really think they want to take the Dryden name off the title."

"Because of the rumors about the plane crash." Amy had come to the same conclusion that had been obvious to a lot of people in the offices of Dryden-Marsdale.

"Even if they're not true, yeah."

Chloe chewed on her lip, listening to what was being said, then cutting to the chase. "But what about the other holdings, in mine, Sophie and Amy's names?"

"That's your choice, but I'd suggest we all sell, give ourselves a clean start."

"It's your job though," Amy pointed out and touched his arm. "I know you wanted to write, or be a teacher, that Dad's company wasn't your choice of a career, but how much would you be giving up?"

That was an easy question to answer. "Nothing. It's not what I want to do. I could give it up for myself, but you need to agree with what you want to do. I mean, if either of you wants to work in corporate finance, then that is something we would deal with."

"No." Amy side-eyed Chloe.

Chloe grimaced, always the free spirit, the artist who told everyone who would listen that she was going to travel the world as soon as she could. "Hell no."

"What about Sophie?"

Amy had a point. What about Sophie? Who could tell if a young child could one day, be a genius with numbers as their dad had been? She wasn't showing signs of it yet, but still, it was a possibility.

Corey sighed noisily. He hated that he was being asked to make decisions on his little sister's behalf. "I genuinely don't think we have a choice here. I think the board want us to bow out gracefully before they decide for us."

"We should be so pissed at this," Chloe snapped. "That is Dad's company. He built it, and now they want his memory erased?"

Corey took her hand. "Nothing will erase Dad's memory or Mom's, okay? We'll take the money and make something new."

"Then do it," Amy said.

A noise outside the car drew Corey's attention. Daniel

was leading a big bay horse into the front yard and stopping far enough away that Corey thought he'd hoped he wouldn't be noticed. Something flared inside Corey. Pleasure? Nervous anticipation? Guilt? Sadness?

Seeing Daniel reminded Corey that he had more to say.

"Amy, Chloe, this ranch is a safe space, okay? There are a lot of people here who need to feel as if they aren't being watched or made to talk. Are we cool with that?"

Amy unbuckled her belt and opened the door. "Yep. I read up on this place. It's cool."

Chloe followed her, and then Corey until all three stood outside. Corey locked the car and watched Daniel lead the horse, walking back the way he'd come. He felt inexplicably sad that Daniel didn't want to say hello, but he guessed there was time to work on that.

"Let's get inside. You can meet the guys."

As soon as he stepped into the cool interior of the ranch house, into the spacious kitchen, he felt at home, and the weight of all his worries slipped away.

"Carrots," Jason announced from the table. "Thank god, you're back. They're running wild in the gardens."

That was the only comment Corey received concerning where he'd been for a few weeks. He could take that. The girls settled in quickly, working the garden with him and Sophie, joke-complaining about digging mud and tending to runaway carrots. Sophie darting from one place to another, clearly in her element.

Maybe the four of them should sell the house, buy a ranch? He noticed Amy checking her nails and saw her grimace at the state of them.

*Maybe not a ranch then.*

There was barbecue food at dinner, and the invite was open to the Dryden family to stay. Corey engineered it, so he ended up sitting by Daniel. This was his chance, but all he could do was flail hopelessly and attempt to find an opening line to begin a conversation. The silence between them was awkward as Daniel looked right at him.

*Say something you freaking idiot.* He berated himself.

Daniel's lips thinned. Then he huffed and walked away, disappearing around the back of the barn with his plate of food.

No one else seemed to notice Daniel leaving. Jason and Amy were talking music, Chloe and Sophie chatting quietly over chicken and corn, so Corey casually stood and sauntered the way Daniel had gone.

He found him soon enough, sitting on a bale of hay, watching the horses, his plate next to him, food untouched.

"Hey." Corey waited for Daniel to side-eye him, or talk, or even stand and move away. He did none of those, steadily watching the horses. Corey couldn't decide whether to stay or go, so he channeled his innate stubbornness and stayed, taking a seat on the next bale over.

"You don't have to talk to me," Daniel said. "I get it's hard."

Corey put down the chicken he was just about to eat.

"It's not hard for me," Corey denied, then sighed noisily. "Yes, it is."

"Told you that."

"Only because I worry you think my sisters know what happened, or that they'll talk to you, or that my uncle was a monster, or that I think we're selling our stake in my parents' company, and hell, whether I should have handed all the information the PI collected over to the cops."

"Maybe you should."

"What would that solve? The plane crash investigation was closed. Everyone who knew my parents can grieve for real now, my sisters included, and my uncle is dead. He's dead, and the only people I'd hurt now would be you guys and my sisters."

"And you."

Corey half-turned on his bale and looked at Daniel. "And me what?" He'd apparently lost the thread of the conversation somewhere.

"If it came out about what your uncle did, what do you think would happen to you?"

Corey closed his eyes briefly. "I'm not sure I really care what people think as long as my sisters are okay."

"You're quite some hero, aren't you?" There was no sarcasm in Daniel's tone, and when Corey opened his eyes, he wasn't sneering at Corey. Actually, he had moved on his bale to face him head on and looked more curious than anything else.

"No."

"Looking out for your sisters, coming to find me at college to shut down anything I knew that might make them vulnerable to hate. I would have liked someone in my life who did that for me."

Corey's breath caught, and his chest was tight. Daniel clearly didn't realize that he'd become someone on the patented 'Corey's list of 'people to look out for,' and he wasn't sure that now was a good time to explain that.

So he changed the subject. "Do you live here?"

"Came for a short visit; haven't left yet. Been here a month, and I'm staying until they tell me to go, or until I'm ready to go." Daniel reached for a chip. He didn't eat it but broke it systematically into tiny pieces as he carried on talking. "I wasn't going to stop here at all, but I know I could make something of myself here. Legacy is wide and open, and I'm my own man. I can set my own hours, even if I have to try not to work too hard. I want to cover some office things eventually, but for now, I'm finding my place in the world."

"And it doesn't worry you that my uncle won't publicly pay for what he did to you?"

"He's dead. So he kind of did already," Daniel murmured.

Grief poked at Corey. It appeared at the weirdest times, but this was because he was reminded his parents were gone, as absolutely final as his uncle. He shoved it back.

"You must detest my family," Corey murmured. "Hate me."

"None of what happened was down to you, and I don't hate you. If anything, I like you more than I should."

Then he picked up his plate and left the barn, and this time, Corey didn't follow him.

## Chapter Eleven

SPRING CAME FAST AND HARD TO LEGACY RANCH. DANIEL had spent four years in Denver at college, stayed in a hostel there in the summer, and had gotten used to the cooler summers. Then his three months in an air-conditioned office had lulled him into a false sense of security. None of that had readied him for the heat he'd grown up with.

Texas heat was brutal at first, but after the first few days, he slipped into a routine of working on the ranch in the coolness of the morning, and finally, he came to terms with the kind of work he could do inside during the heat of the day.

He didn't work in the office with Kyle. He couldn't quite bring himself to share space with someone else yet. Even if Kyle was out of the place more often than not.

Kyle didn't expect him to work in there and was happy to let Daniel set up a desk area in his own small room. When he worked, he propped open his door and thanked the heavens his room faced north, so the sun wasn't quite so cruel. He'd stopped using the small air-con unit because he got too cold. It was as if he couldn't win.

Weeks of staying here had turned into three months, and when he woke each morning, he felt as if he could accomplish something useful.

Sometimes the nightmares visited him, but most nights, he had dreams that were less about the angel rescuing him, and more about the horses and the land that was consuming his thoughts.

His newest inspiration had begun two weeks back when he'd heard Kyle say he couldn't get a grip on how to add some photos to the website.

Daniel knew coding well enough to go into the Legacy website and add the photos for him. That led to him seeing that none of the images on there were being handled properly and none linked through to more information. Not to mention Legacy Ranch had no social media presence. Then he realized most of the information was out of date, and no one at Legacy knew what they wanted a website for. The people who came here remained anonymous, but how did they find Legacy in the first place if they weren't referred there?

He set about finding out what purpose it served, and at first, this involved asking simple questions, but soon it burned in him that this needed to be *right*. He wanted the site to be a place that not only provided information but became a source of knowledge about all kinds of things. Horses. Outreach. GLBTQ issues. Legal shit. Finances.

So the website became his first project.

Horses in the morning, website work in the afternoon.

And every weekend, Corey.

Since he'd said that stupid shit about liking Corey, the

weekends had become stupidly awkward whenever he saw him. He knew he was way more in tune with Sophie than he was with her brother. It wasn't that he didn't have things to talk about with Corey. There were the horses. Or the website. Or the ranch. But the elephant in the room, or stable, or kitchen, or wherever they were avoiding contact, was the connection between them, and the weight of it was taking its toll.

Because of this, Daniel woke up on the sunny Texas Saturday and didn't want to go outside in case he saw Corey. The decision wasn't even one he consciously made, but when he opened the door and looked out, he knew he couldn't leave his room.

This was a significant obstacle, and he wasn't sure how he was going to get over it. After all, he simply needed to step over the threshold and carry on about his day. How could something that easy be such an enormous block?

He opened the door again. It didn't help that the Dryden car was arriving, along with what he presumed would be Corey and his sisters. Amy was lovely, open, warm and easily affectionate. Which scared the shit out of him. Chloe was prickly and didn't like touching random people. That; that he was happy with. It was Sophie though who unmanned him, asking him questions about his life as if he was completely normal and not a fraud.

Then there was Corey and that damned elephant.

He watched all four of them get out of the car, Chloe and Amy chatting, Sophie sprinting straight for the kitchen, and then there was Corey. *Looking this way.*

He waved and waited, probably thinking that Daniel was just about to leave his room.

So Daniel did what he had to do.

Shut the door in Corey's face.

Then in shame, he slid down to sit on the floor and prayed to anyone who would listen to make Corey go away.

When there was a knock, he knew it would be Corey. Daniel knew, just like in the dorm that time, that Corey wouldn't leave. Persistence was one of Corey's *things*.

"Are you coming in for breakfast?" Corey asked, loud enough for Daniel to hear.

Daniel curled in on himself, in his usual protective stance, and then realized abruptly that it wasn't working. It didn't matter how small the ball was that he wound himself into, the problems, issues, and lies that spun around Corey and Daniel wouldn't go away.

*Why isn't this working?*

"Daniel? Are you okay? Should I get someone? Kyle maybe?"

*Great. That is the last thing I need.*

He rolled to his feet, scowled at the reflection he saw in the mirror, all flushed and stupid looking, and then ripped open his door. Corey took a step back in surprise, his hand still up from where Daniel assumed he'd be knocking again.

And the floodgates holding back Daniel's emotions and fears opened. "I do like you, and I was hoping maybe we'd be friends, but I can't look at you and not think that you're afraid to talk to me. I know what your uncle did was shit." He inhaled sharply. "It was worse than that. It was cruel and nasty, and what he and others did has changed my life forever. That doesn't mean we can't talk like real adults, because he was nothing to do with you, and you are nothing to do with what happened back then. I want to be someone new, and the more you won't look at me in a normal manner since I said I liked you, the more I refuse to talk to you, and then it's a whole shitfest of crap."

"Daniel—"

"Let me finish."

"Sorry."

"And stop that apologizing shit. I'm done with that. I like you, okay. You seem as if you're a nice guy, and it would be cool to talk about horses, and the ranch, and the work I'm doing without referencing it all back to the nightmares of my freaking childhood." Daniel was working up a head of steam now, and he couldn't fail to notice Corey taking a step back. Just that small movement, indicating that Corey wanted to leave, had Daniel holding out a hand to stop him. Of course, he was too far away to reach, but the gesture was enough to get Corey to stop.

*What do I say now?*

Corey surprised him, moving toward his hand and then shaking it firmly. "Hi, my name is Corey. I work here on the weekends in the garden. It's nice to meet you."

Daniel felt the warmth of another man's touch, and he didn't recoil, and that was amazing in itself.

"Hi," he began quietly. Then he forced some energy into his words. "I'm Daniel. I work in the barns with the horses and do some office things as well. I live here. It's good to meet you, too."

That had been six weeks ago and now they'd gone from being wary and avoiding each other to talking all the time. From horses to websites and everything in between.

Last weekend had been an exception, but Daniel didn't

let it deter him or make him think he'd fucked up. He simply asked Corey what was wrong because Corey had been quiet. That was taking their friendship to a different level, one where it was obvious Daniel cared about Corey's welfare.

"We have some decisions to make at home," Corey had explained. But just saying that was enough to make Daniel smile.

They sat for the longest time on the hay bales just shooting the breeze, and it was nice to have a friend who knew what had happened to him but didn't want to talk about it. He'd never told anyone else, never let anyone, but he'd never had to tell Corey.

Today, when he'd woken up, he'd been excited about the day ahead, something that was becoming more frequent, and a lot of times it was to do with Corey. Or Amy, who had taken to following Daniel around when he worked. She was cool, had a boyfriend called Michael who seemed to be the center of her world, and kept saying one weekend she'd bring him out here if that was okay with everyone.

Daniel reassured her it was okay with him, but she needed to check with Kyle. Knowing Kyle, he wouldn't have said no either, and so this morning, with it being Saturday, he expected that possibly Michael would turn up with the Dryden siblings in their fancy-ass car.

He wasn't wrong. Michael was a smiling, happy, confident guy, who fell into the swing of things immediately. Of course, that meant Amy wasn't following him around so much, but that didn't matter, because this led to it being him and Corey alone in the barn, on the bales, with lunch.

"Big week this week," Corey announced before either of them began to eat. Daniel took a bite of the huge ham roll and waited for more information. "Signed the paperwork and banked the money. Dryden-Marsdale is now just Marsdale Finance."

Daniel chewed, then swallowed. "Are you okay with that?"

Corey had spoken about their parents' company, about how much it meant, on several occasions. Each time he recounted his worries, he sounded less sad, and today, he appeared positively happy about everything. What a difference time made.

Corey smiled at him. A wide grin that made his eyes crinkle at the corners and exposed a dimple that Daniel frequently focused on.

"It's a relief for all of us. Well, everyone but Sophie, who isn't overly concerned about any of it."

"Must be nice to be a kid," Daniel observed.

"We still have the house, and it's a beautiful house, a home at the moment for all of us. No one can make us leave the memories we have there. One day maybe we'll all be gone, and it will be someone else's forever home, but for now, we still see our parents in every line of it."

Corey settled back on the bale and pulled his legs up to sit cross-legged, and warmth spread through Daniel. He loved smiling, relaxed Corey.

He wanted to hug smiling, relaxed Corey.

And kiss him.

*Maybe*.

"Earth to Daniel." Corey's voice broke into his thoughts. "What's got you so serious? Don't worry about us. We'll be fine."

"I wasn't thinking about that. It was more other things in my head." He took another bite of sandwich and chewed as he thought about how to word what he wanted to ask. "I've been at Legacy a while now, and I realized I listen to you talk about the house and the city, and I haven't seen either."

"That's easily arranged. Come back with us tonight, stay. There is plenty of room, and I can bring you back tomorrow."

"No." The reply was instinctive, even though Daniel really wanted to say yes. "Not yet. One day I will."

"It's all good."

"I was thinking, maybe you wanted to go for a ride with me later when it's cooler. After dinner?"

"I'd like that."

Daniel looked back down at what remained of his sandwiches, opening one and pulling out the meat. He liked to deconstruct carefully built lunches and eat the parts separately. Last weekend, he'd done the same thing with the pizza they'd had for dinner. Pulling off the pepperoni and putting it to one side, and Corey had commented on it. Daniel liked saving the best bits for last, which a few nights back led to him having an eerily real dream about sex.

With Corey.

Which was, on the one hand, freaking fantastic, and on the other, made Daniel feel as if he really needed to talk to Corey before things got out of control. He steeled himself for complete rejection.

"Can I ask you a question?"

Corey looked over and smiled reassuringly. He did that a lot, laughed and was encouraging, and supportive, and according to Daniel's dreams, he was also good in bed. *Damn good in bed.*

"Anything."

"That's a dangerous guideline to give a man." Daniel realized abruptly he was teasing Corey. That was a nice feeling. "I wanted to know if you had a boyfriend, and if not, would you consider a date. With me."

Corey put the lettuce he was holding back onto the plate.

"Yes." He showed no hesitation. "I mean, no, I don't have anyone, and yes, a date would be good, and hey, we could start tonight with the horses."

Daniel smiled because Corey was adorable when he was confused and messed up like this. It only usually happened when Gabriel teased Corey. He went back to his sandwich.

"How about sex?"

Corey coughed on the lettuce he'd swallowed and banged a hand to his chest. "Jesus, warn a guy."

Daniel waited until Corey had drunk his water, and then until he'd made a big show of righting his plate on his lap. Then he pushed harder.

"So, sex."

Corey opened his mouth to say something and then stopped. "What about it?" he asked.

"I think about it with you, sometimes. And I know that it's fucked-up to say that, and I get that I don't have the social niceties that go with conventional courtship."

"I love that you just used 'courtship' in a sentence," Corey blurted and then wrinkled his nose. "Keep going. My bad."

Daniel shook his head in feigned dismay. "I want a

connection, so one day, if things went well, I'd like to think that you and I could...you know."

"Bump uglies?" Corey suggested.

"Yeah, but I might... Look, I want to be upfront here, okay? I know that you've probably got all this stuff in your head about me, and what happened, and how it's part of me, which it is, but not so that you have to worry, and I want to get over some of my shit, and work on getting past things, with you."

He stopped because God knew where all that was coming from.

*Probably from one dream where we were on my bed, and I was this close to coming inside Corey.*

Corey was quiet, and he'd gone from smiling to serious, and Daniel got the feeling that somehow he'd fucked up in that wild vomit of information.

Corey stood and stretched, left his plate where it was, and nodded at Daniel. "I'll see you later."

For a moment Daniel sat absolutely still and willed Corey not to leave, and then he had an epiphany that he shouldn't do that. Regular guys went after what they wanted. Right?

"Corey, wait." He abandoned his lunch and caught up with Corey just before he walked outside, catching his arm and holding him to stop him from leaving. He looked so serious as he pulled free.

"I'm not sure this is a good idea," Corey said, his tone even.

"Shit, what did I say?" Daniel scrubbed his eyes. "What did I do wrong? You have to explain."

"You said you wanted someone like me to help you get over your past. That's right, isn't it?"

"What? No. I didn't say that, or at least I didn't…"

This was why he didn't talk about real stuff. This was why his hookups at college had been nameless and brief.

"I think I'll wait," Corey said when Daniel had run out of words.

"Wait? For what?"

"I can't be the temporary one who fixes what you think is broken."

"Corey, I didn't mean—"

"I think I could want more," Corey said. He reached out to Daniel then, cradled his face with both hands, his thumbs tracing Daniel's cheekbones, and regarded him steadily. He leaned closer, and for one shining, horrific, tempting moment Daniel thought Corey may kiss him. His lips parted. He wanted to taste Corey, to know him better. And there was silence as Corey stopped moving and half-closed his eyes.

This was it. This was going to be Daniel's first real kiss.

"Corey! Where are you!" Sophie's shout broke the silence.

Corey released his hold and backed away. "Here Sophie," he called back and stepped into the sunshine.

Daniel went back for their plates, then sat down, a little more than dazed and a whole lot thoughtful. There had definitely been an almost-kiss. He'd got to be the age he was, and he'd never kissed anyone before.

That was so much more intimate than fucking someone or being fucked. It was a deliberate decision to touch someone in a way that left a person vulnerable. Or at least left him feeling that way.

All the bravado he'd used to front that huge

conversation was slipping away, slowly, then faster until everything felt like shit.

"Hey," someone said to him, and he looked up to see Corey had returned and stood in front of him. He didn't have the words to talk right then, but he didn't need to. Corey leaned down and kissed him. Nothing passionate, but not cold. A press of his lips against Daniel's. Then he stepped back. "Just in case you thought I wasn't interested. See you at dinner." He ruffled Daniel's short hair and left then, and when Daniel's face began to hurt, he didn't realize why at first.

Then it hit him.

He couldn't stop smiling.

---

Daniel had a horse. At least that's how Kyle had put it after Daniel had been at Legacy for a couple of weeks.

*His horse.*

"This is Hennessy. She's your horse now," Kyle had said.

All Daniel could think at that time was he wasn't even sure he was staying at Legacy. In fact, he had it in his mind that it was probably time to move on. Head north, away from Texas, and to find a job on another ranch instead of more office work. Wyoming maybe? Or Montana? Seemed as if ranch work was something he was good at, and he did love horses.

Then slowly, before he'd even realized it was happening, he got used to Legacy, and to having a horse, and to Corey and his sisters visiting at the weekends. Familiar with being able to be himself around Kyle and

Liam, understood by Jason, to laugh with Gabriel, and to be loved unconditionally by Hennessy, who followed him everywhere as much as she could, when he was out working on the fencing or clearing the fields.

He ate dinner. That much he remembered. Helped himself to a single beer, and a couple of water bottles plus the cookies that everyone seemed to bake and that he'd become addicted to. Then slipped them into a backpack which he put over his shoulders. He moved away from the food and saddled Hennessy, nuzzling her white mane, a shocking contrast to her black-and-gray coat.

"We have things to do tonight," he murmured and steadied her when she skipped sideways and nudged him along with her. She loved to play, and he adored her for it.

*It would be hard to give her up.*

He'd asked permission from Jason to borrow Mistry and saddled her up as well, and then there was nothing to do except wait. He didn't have to hang around long because Corey seemed as eager as him to get going, and before he knew it, they were away from the ranch, heading up to the bluff, riding in companionable silence. Dusk loaned a mauve hue to the sky, and the dark boulders strewn across the ground cast weird shadows on the path. He knew exactly where he was going, a place he'd found a couple weeks back, where a rocky outcrop offered a beautiful view of the land around them. It was the perfect place to talk, eat cookies, and drink.

*Who said romance was dead?*

His thoughts tripped him up. This wasn't romance. This was a chance to get to know Corey away from the ranch, to work on their budding friendship.

*But he kissed you.*

He indicated that they leave the main path, and Mistry followed Hennessy's lead, walking onto the hard-packed dirt and upward to the top of the bluff.

"It's beautiful up here. I can't remember the last time I was on a horse. I was fourteen or so, I guess." Corey rambled on about horses and parties, and the time he'd been thrown into a bush, and wasn't it fortunate there was a bush, and how his dad had rescued him, and his mom had fussed over him. Everything sounded utterly ordinary, and Daniel didn't want him to stop talking about that *normal* of his, but at the same time, he wanted him to stop talking about family and memories that were so fucking golden and perfect.

Instead, he focused on where they were heading and gauging how quickly they would get there. And the ants were inside him, the acid-hot ants that pricked his memories and made him feel restless and uncoordinated. The closer they got, the more the memories he was trying to push back forced themselves to the front of his head.

This was a date. Right? This was Daniel putting himself out there to be touched and hurt, and maybe have his heart broken. This was big. Huge. This was life-changing and possibly soul-destroying, and then his chest tightened, and his breath hitched, and he bent over Hennessy's back, cursing his stupid *fucking* brain.

He felt a hand on his back, Hennessy moving sideways, the brush of Corey's leg against his, and the soft but insistent use of his name. Corey was asking if he was okay, and humiliatingly, he wasn't okay. He was tired and stressed, and the perfect idea he'd had of this date was twisting in the wind.

"It's important you know some stuff," he blurted when

his spiraling thoughts refused to be contained any longer. He looked sideways and saw the concern in Corey's expression.

"Okay," Corey encouraged when Daniel was quiet for a while.

Hennessy nickered and shook her mane, and for a second Daniel was right in the moment and saw they were exactly where he wanted them to be. Somehow, that gave him strength, and he pushed himself upright, then slid from Hennessy's back.

"We're here," he announced and tied up Hennessy and then Mistry after Corey dismounted. He took off his backpack and clambered up the rocks to the sitting place. Corey didn't argue. He followed him and then waited as Daniel spread a blanket over a smooth indentation that formed a seat of sorts.

"I brought beer or water," he said, opening the backpack and peering in. "Just one beer though, sorry."

"Water is good," Corey said, and that one stupid small decision was enough for Daniel to begin to relax again. "So what is the important stuff I need to know?" Corey asked gently as he unscrewed the top of his water.

*Oh. That. Yep, I said that.*

"Little things I guess.; I say things wrong sometimes, when I'm not thinking straight, and I sometimes have moments when…the past sneaks in."

"It's fine. We're good."

"Just like that, you say 'we're good'?"

Corey capped the water and pulled his legs toward him, resting his hands on his knees. He looked calm and thoughtful, and then he smiled, and the smile was beautiful. "I like you, Danny. A lot. I think you might feel the same way. So. We should kiss, and talk, and look at the view, and just see what happens. Life is too short to walk away from all its possibilities."

"You called me Danny."

"Shit." Corey felt guilty. Had he fucked up? "Sorry."

"No, I like it. Some people called me Danny at college. It felt normal." He gestured to the world beyond their small part of it. "I want to feel normal."

"Then I'll call you that all the time."

Daniel returned the smile. "Okay then. Cookie?"

"Is it one of Jason's?"

Daniel pulled out the small container. "Yep."

"The ones with the extra chocolate?"

"Think so."

Corey helped himself to one of the cookies and bit into it, making all kinds of obscene noises as he crunched and chewed, and finally swallowed his first bite. Daniel felt something shift inside him. If nothing else happened, he realized he was at peace sitting here with Corey. That was a big thing. He experimentally touched Corey's knee and then edged a little closer when Corey laced a hand with his and held firm.

"I love being here with you, Danny," Corey murmured.

"Back at ya," Daniel said. Leaning into Corey felt good. When they kissed it was gentle, and together they watched the sunset.

## Chapter Twelve

THE FINAL DAY IN THE OFFICE WAS EMOTIONAL. COREY leaving the company his dad had worked so hard to create, but it was the physical things that were hard. His dad's files, the pens in his dad's drawer, the half-finished book of Sudoku puzzles, all of which he scooped into the box that Patricia, his dad's former PA, had given him.

"What about this?" Chloe asked, holding up a certificate of attendance from some training course. Their dad's name was front and center, and Corey took it from her. Reno Finance Conference, 1999.

Corey would only have been six or so then, and Sophie wouldn't have even been born. She might like to see the kind of things their father had learned, and he added it to the folder of paperwork he was taking.

Patricia had told him the room was empty of anything to do with the company, and that everything left was personal; told Chloe and him that they could take whatever they wanted. The box was small but filled to bursting with paperwork, folders, and photos. Not to mention the pens from his desk and the puzzle book. The safe in the wall was open, empty of contents, and the fade marks around where the finance certificate had hung were starkly visible.

There wasn't anything of their father here, not the man they loved, that was all back at the house. Seeing the safe though, reminded him that back home there was another safe in their parents' room. He recalled that there had been paperwork in there, but everything had been pulled out. In fact, he was sure that it had been Amy who had been searching for their wedding certificate for the lawyer.

*Where has that stuff gone? Is it all in Dad's home office? Amy will know.* It could be in the things she'd moved. There would be other things like the certificate that painted a picture of the kind of man their dad had been.

"Ready?" Chloe asked. She did a full three-sixty of the room, and Corey was relieved that on this Sunday morning the office was empty of other staff. With the floor-to-ceiling glass, everyone would've been able to see that Chloe hadn't managed any of this without crying or that he'd stood like an idiot for a good ten minutes just breathing in the air trapped in the room.

He picked up the box, hefted it until he had a good hold, and nodded. This was the last time he'd stand there, and it was yet another connection severed at the moment the plane crashed. Tilting his chin, he indicated the light, and it was Chloe who turned it off and shut the door behind them. He could see the name *Edward Dryden* on the glass or at least the shadow left by the removal of the silver letters. They might have scraped it away, but no one could erase the fact yet that their dad had worked there once, and that it had been his baby.

"Bye, Dad," Chloe murmured and called the elevator.

They went down to the basement, loaded the things they'd collected into the car, and left the building without looking back. One more painful thing done.

"What about the house?" Chloe asked as they joined the slow-moving Sunday traffic to head home. "Do you think we should sell it as well?"

"Do you want to?" Corey hadn't even thought about the house. It was all paid for, and it kept his family together.

"No, but…" She stopped talking, and he glanced at her. She had her lower lip between her teeth, always a sign she was thinking hard.

"But what?"

It would break his heart if the girls wanted the house gone, only because right now he couldn't imagine living anywhere else.

"Amy had a letter from Oxford, offering a place for her Masters."

"She did?" Why was this the first time he heard this? He knew she'd applied to work and live in the UK, and that the chances of her going had been good. She'd worked hard on her application, and she knew what she wanted to study. Her moving to England for a short while had always been in her future. He guessed he'd thought she'd change her mind, given all the things that had happened, and that she seemed so happy with Michael.

"Yeah, she wasn't going to tell anyone, but I needed to borrow stuff, and I found it."

"You snooped on her?"

Chloe huffed. "She left it out. I didn't exactly look for it. So I told her I'd seen it, and she went all weird. Said it wasn't time to leave right now, that the house needed us all, that we all had to have each other. You need to talk to her."

"Me?" He shot Chloe another look, aghast at the concept of talking to Amy about life choices. That was Mom's job.

*Had been Mom's job.*

"You need to tell her it's okay to go, that the house is a place, that we'll be fine on our own, and that I'll stay with you and Sophie."

All Corey could think was that Chloe was also coming to the time in her life when she had decisions to make and that it might just be him and Sophie soon. He didn't say that though. Instead, he did what every good parent would do.

"I'll tell her. Have you decided which college you are going to?"

Chloe said nothing, which was telling. Corey didn't push her, concentrated on driving and waiting her out.

"Denver, maybe." He saw her noncommittal shrug in his peripheral vision.

"That was where Daniel went. You should talk to him. He can give you all the best places to go."

Corey didn't actually know if this was true or not, but it kept Chloe talking, and that was a good thing.

"I'll ask him, but I haven't decided if I'm going yet."

"What? Why wouldn't you go?"

Chloe huffed. "We're not all college brats, you know. I was talking to Kyle yesterday about social work, and he said I should talk to Steve in the city, about maybe working with him."

College had always been Corey's aim, same as Amy, and he needed to rethink his life view for this, but if there was one thing that he'd learned over the last year, everyone had their own path.

"Sounds good," he said.

"So, the house, are we selling it? Because…" She twisted her hands in her lap. "I don't want to yet, if that matters. But I don't want to live here either. None of this makes sense in my head."

He reached over and covered her hands. "Of course it matters. I agree we should keep it, for at least a while. For us all."

When they got back, Amy and Sophie were waiting, ready to go to Legacy, but as they all bundled into the car, after he'd deposited the box in the home office, Corey pulled Amy to one side. He hugged her tight, and she hugged him back before extricating herself.

He didn't hang around. "So, Amy, you got accepted at Oxford."

Amy's mouth fell open, and she stared right at Chloe. "She told you."

"She didn't have to," Corey lied. "I remember it was about now you should have been hearing. Chloe just confirmed what I already thought."

She punched him on the arm. "You're a terrible liar, Corey Dryden."

"I have just one thing to say to you," Corey said and grabbed the offending fist, pulling her in for another hug. "Mom and Dad would have been so proud, and I'll help you pack."

She hugged him tighter. "That's two things."

"Will you go?" He wanted that to be a statement where he told her she had to go, but it had come out as a question, despite his best efforts.

"What about the girls? The house? What about what you need?"

He eased her away and placed his hands on her shoulders. "I'm want to stay in this house a little longer, for me, for Sophie, and I want to work more with Legacy somehow. Maybe with Daniel? Who knows, but what I do know is that I *want* those things, Amy. As much as I want you to go to England and start the next part of your life."

She searched his face, probably looking for any chink in his armor, but how could she? He did want to stay in this house. He loved the idea of being there for Sophie, to be a kind of pseudo-father. He wanted to work with Legacy on something that made a difference.

And the one thing he'd left off the list.

He wanted to be with Daniel.

And hoped that Daniel wanted him back.

"Okay," she murmured.

That was it done.

---

They made it to Legacy late because of the office emptying, and at first, Corey couldn't find Daniel, and he felt restless with the need to see him.

Finally, he checked in the one place he hadn't expected to find Daniel; his room. The door was wide open, which was Corey's first clue, and Daniel was at his desk with a sketchpad in front of him, along with an array of colored pens. The pens were laid out in rainbow order, missing the green, which Daniel had in his hand.

"Hey," Corey said from the door, and Daniel looked up at him and smiled.

"Wanna see?" he asked and gestured for Corey to come into the room. This was the first time he'd set foot into Daniel's space, and it felt as if he'd been offered the most significant privilege and expression of trust.

On the sheet was a plan of Legacy, hand-drawn and, the detail of the buildings and the roads were scarily accurate. Daniel had begun to shade in a green space, the front of the main house, and pods, and tapped his pen there.

"I wanted something to refer to when I worked on plans and thought maybe Sophie would be interested in working on extending the garden. Maybe grow flowers as well as vegetables." He pushed over a picture, a quintessential English country garden, and nodded at it. "Not those plants of course. They'd last two seconds in the heat, but this mix of color looks so cool."

And for the second time today, an indefinable *thing* eased inside Corey. As if he wasn't wary of touching Daniel, as if it was okay. He rested a hand gently on Daniel's shoulder and leaned in a little. Not too far, but enough to be *there*.

"Looks good, and I'm sure she'll love it."

Daniel stretched and stood up. "Coffee, all the coffee, and cookies," he announced.

Corey could no more help himself than he could not eat a plate of Jason's cookies. He cradled Daniel's face and kissed him. They hadn't moved much past lazy exploration and always for short bursts, but this time, Daniel evidently wanted more. He locked his hands around the back of Corey's neck and tilted his head a little to deepen the kiss.

This was so right. The warmth of a Texas day, the light from the skylights, and the buzz of need that he was sure they both felt. He slid his hands from face to shoulders and then down Daniel's sides until he rested his hold on Daniel's hips. They were both hard, and Corey wanted to take this further. He desperately wanted to place his hands on Daniel's ass and pull him against him. Daniel groaned into the kiss and then extricated himself.

For a moment they looked at each other. Daniel was serious and focused, and then in a quick motion, he was back to kissing, this time holding Corey tighter, and Corey couldn't help that his hands ended up on Daniel's ass, and Daniel didn't object. If anything, his moan was more than arousal, and Corey was right there with him.

"Oh god, Danny," he muttered.

Daniel laughed. "Love it when you call me that," he said into another kiss.

Corey nudged him back so that he was pressed against the desk, and Daniel wriggled to sit on the desk and widen his legs so that Corey could stand between them. The kiss was heated, and if this had been anywhere else, their bluff they'd ridden to for three weekends in a row, or in here, but with the door shut, then maybe it would have gone further. Right now, Corey wanted to see Daniel, to kiss more than his lips, taste his skin from throat to toe and all the interesting, exciting places between.

But this wasn't the right place or time, and reluctantly they separated. Daniel caught him as he stepped back. "It's weird, you know," he murmured.

"What is?

"That I want more."

They kissed once more, and then Corey sketched a wave. "Later."

He had to go, to get away from the temptation. He

hunted down Jason, who always had cookies, and walked straight into a good-natured debate between Jason, Sophie, and a newly arrived Gabriel about how many carrots Legacy needed to grow.

"A million." Sophie finished her argument and crossed her arms over her chest.

Jason roughed her hair, and she pummeled him until he called uncle. Through all of it, Gabriel looked on with a wide grin, and Corey watched from the door.

Sophie would remember her parents. Her older siblings would remind her when she felt as if she lost a connection, but right now, this was what she needed. Legacy was her second home.

He helped himself to coffee, pouted at the lack of cookies and then wandered back out to the garden. What had started as a nebulous idea the first day he'd visited had become something tangible. Asparagus, beets, the ubiquitous carrots, and a mix of potatoes that broke up the soil.

Today was high tunnel building day, a project that Gabriel had suggested. Everything was there already, and he rolled out the easy-to-follow plans. Gabriel appeared a little later. They needed to dig a base, and that was possibly the only hard work involved, and even that didn't take long. Particularly when Daniel joined them and began digging up his third of the hard soil and laying down a pathway that would run down the center of the tunnel. Daniel and Gabriel were at one end, but Corey could hear them talking about all kind of things.

About life, about Gabriel's partner, Cameron, and Cameron's hotel in the city. Yep, he owned a hotel, a complete hotel—that blew Daniel's mind. Gabriel even began a conversation about football. Although that conversation didn't last long, as neither were huge fans. Corey lost himself in the constant, repetitive digging, only stopping briefly for water, and didn't realize how serious the conversation between Gabriel and Daniel had become.

"Yeah," Gabriel answered a question that Daniel had clearly asked. "Kyle talks about a guy called Paul, in a suit, but I don't remember a Paul or the description."

Daniel stopped working. "I have Frank. Do you remember that name?"

Gabriel shook his head and crouched down to ease a hard-as-stone chunk of earth out of the way of the path. "Not from then, no," he replied enigmatically. Corey didn't know Gabriel's full story since he'd gotten away from the Bar Five, but he had heard hints from Kyle and Jason when they'd all been talking. He knew that Gabriel had been a guy who made money through sex, and that it hadn't always been his decision, and that someone had controlled him. It sounded horrific, and how Gabriel had come through it all, Corey didn't know. Nor Kyle and Daniel, for that matter.

"Frank was the one who—" Daniel stopped, and he didn't restart.

Gabriel didn't push, and Corey pretended he hadn't heard any of it. All he knew was that Daniel was skittish for the remainder of the project, a little too quiet, and unable to look Corey in the eye or exchange smiles.

By the time dinner had come, Corey knew something was very wrong. Corey and the girls always left around six on a Sunday to get Sophie back to school, but when they were going, there was no sign of Daniel in the kitchen, where he usually waited to say goodbye.

Corey found Kyle in the office and knocked on the door.

"I can't find Danny," he said, reverting to the nickname he'd taken to calling Daniel when they were alone.

Kyle pulled himself from his spreadsheets and looked up at him, blinking as he processed what he'd been told.

"Did you check to see if he's in with the horses?"

"Of course I did. I looked everywhere, but he's always in the kitchen when we go."

"Check with the horses again."

"No, you're not listening, Kyle. Eight weeks now, and he's always in the kitchen to say goodbye on a Sunday. He sneaks Sophie cookies, and we hug, and he's not here."

Kyle frowned. "What happened?"

"He was talking to Gabriel earlier, and he's been weirded out this afternoon, and now he's not here to say goodbye."

Kyle switched off his PC and stood, grabbing his hat and jacket. "We got this," he said.

"I don't like this. I want to find him."

"Get the girls home. We've got this."

"Kyle—"

Kyle gripped his shoulders, and his expression was one of compassion. "We've got this. Go home. I'll call you."

"I don't want to go home until I've seen him."

"That isn't what he needs right now. Be normal. Don't change what you do because he needs to be apart from us. I've seen this before. Hell, I've done this before. Get home, and I'll call you."

Corey's chest filled with emotion. How could he explain how he felt? What words did he use that made any sense of the panic he was feeling? How he made it home, he didn't know. Sophie was chatting and asking why Daniel didn't have cookies for her, and Amy and Chloe were discussing boys, and music and it was a mess of noise. They arrived home, but Corey didn't get out of the car.

"Amy, can you stay here with Sophie?"

Amy glanced over at him, and her laughing expression faded. "What's wrong?"

"I need to go back to Legacy. I forgot something."

"Cookies!" Sophie shouted.

All of them got out of the car, and Chloe took one look at her brother and grasped Sophie's hand to take her indoors.

"Go, we'll be fine," Amy reassured him.

And Corey was back on the road in an instant.

## Chapter Thirteen

DANIEL WASN'T SURPRISED WHEN SOMEONE FOUND HIM. He'd expected it to be Kyle, but it was Gabriel.

Not that Daniel had been intentionally hiding, but unless someone was looking, he guessed no one would know where he was, so he had to admit part of him wanted to be alone. Daniel knew damn well that he measured his entire self-worth by weird standards. A result of two years of enforced isolation and pain at Bar Five. Counseling had shown him a way forward. He had to find his own validation and purpose. He'd been so close to feeling something for Corey, and then one simple word had thrown everything off course.

*Frank.*

He'd done everything possible to hide what had happened, weighed down with shame, but talking to Gabriel shouldn't be like that. Gabriel had lost way more years to pain than he had and would understand the mess in Daniel's head. So why did his mind abruptly shut down when they'd been talking? He'd seen Corey look at him more than once, probably wanting to ask him if he was okay. This was part of the reason Daniel had run away tonight, determined not to see Corey before the four Dryden siblings left. It was cowardly, and he knew damn well it would have hurt Corey.

He didn't want to hurt him, but if he wanted a romantic relationship to move forward, he had to open up to Corey, and that meant he left himself wide open to possible rejection.

*Can I cope with rejection?*

Gabriel didn't talk, only tied off his horse next to Hennessy, and scrambled to sit up on the bluff. They sat in silence, staring into the dark for the longest time, until Daniel was irritable with the waiting for a lecture from Gabriel, and made a move to leave.

"How did you end up at the Bar Five?" Gabriel said before he could get up entirely.

He huffed. "Jesus, Gabriel, I thought what happened at Bar Five stays there?"

Gabriel shook his head. "Not really. The rest of us talk about it when we need to."

"I don't want or *need* to talk about it."

Silence again.

"You know, there is this accepted thing out there, that every superhero has a good origin story." Gabriel was clearly not dropping this.

"I'm not a freaking superhero." He added a *duh* in his head and hoped that was the end of it. It wasn't.

"Well, whatever, but here's my story."

"I don't want to hear it—"

"So my mom worked at Bar Five, and she died, cancer,

and I was lost in the system. Well, we think that was what happened. How they kept me there was another thing. They broke my knees when I tried to run." He stretched out his legs in front of him and rubbed his thigh. "See how my left leg twists a bit?"

Daniel couldn't see much in the dark. "No," he admitted.

"Well, it does. I knew they had another boy, much younger. You, I guess. I mean, I don't know, but we're closer in age, and, yeah, I think maybe you were there at the same time. I know it all unraveled, but I really want to know how you got away when I couldn't without help."

Daniel recalled the shadow in his dreams, the long hair that slipped over his face, the soft words of warning, and the scent of perfume that followed him into his sleep. He didn't know what had happened. Not to this day could he recall how, one minute he was in the barn where everything happened, to then being in a police precinct wrapped in a bright red blanket and being supported by a cop.

He didn't want to revisit dreams.

"I had help, I think, but I'm not talking about that shit." No one could make him talk about the mistakes he made, and how he'd ended up in hell.

"Sometimes you have to talk, you know, and who better to talk to than someone who's been there."

"Whatever."

*Please go. Please leave.* Please *let me work my way through this on my own.*

But no, Gabriel wasn't letting it lie. "So, go on, tell me. What is *your* origin story?"

Daniel scrubbed at his eyes. "Fuck off," he snarled because hell, he didn't need Gabriel pushing him.

"Okay, you don't want to talk about Bar Five, then tell me what started this need to be alone then? Was it talking about that Frank guy? Is Frank part of how you ended up at Bar Five?"

"And I said, fuck off."

"You can go if you want, and I'll stop asking questions," Gabriel offered.

"I was here first. You go."

Gabriel crossed his legs at his ankles and settled back into the worn stone seat. "I like it here."

Daniel scrambled to sit up, ready to call Gabriel on his crap. "You're an asshole," he said with heat. "A fucking son of a bitch, to rip me apart by asking me that."

Gabriel peered up at him and half-smiled. "I've been accused of worse. Called worse. So tell me about Corey instead, kid."

Daniel could leave now. He would have to clamber over Gabriel, but the guy wasn't anything special, not some big man who could stop him doing what he wanted. His hands curled into fists, and he imagined hitting Gabriel, and how much better that could make him feel. He even lifted a fist to aim and then dropped it and fell back to the stone, mutinous and pissed.

"I'm not a fucking kid," he snapped.

"I guess you're not, so tell me about Corey."

He refused to talk, and then he couldn't hold back what he wanted to say. "Corey's a good man," Daniel offered the lame explanation of what Corey really was.

"Yeah, good, responsible, blah blah. Go on, tell me about *you* and Corey."

"That's none of your business."

Gabriel eased back a little and uncrossed his legs, and Daniel heard his soft huff of pain. It was that small sound that hurt more than the questions. He and Gabriel had a connection in this life that others wouldn't understand. They were outsiders looking in and wanting to be normal. They had a chance here at Legacy, but the ghosts were always there, just over their shoulders waiting to drag them back again.

"I can't," he said miserably.

The *clop* of hooves interrupted them, and Daniel sighed, expecting Kyle or Liam, shocked when it was Corey who dismounted and tied off Mistry.

Gabriel leaned into Daniel and said, so quietly, "Maybe it's Corey you need to tell your origin story to? Seems to me he's a *good man*." Gabriel used his own words against him and scrambled to stand, using the rock as a lever. "You gonna be okay?"

Corey hovered behind them, and Gabriel reached out to grip Daniel's hand. "You're safe here." He went over to the horses, clapping a hand on Corey's shoulder and exchanging soft words before mounting and riding back down the way they'd come.

"What are you doing here?" Daniel asked before coughing to clear his throat of what sounded like an accusation.

"I can go if you want me to," Corey said instantly.

*Please go. No questions about how I'm doing, or what is wrong with me.*

"You don't *have* to go," he said instead.

Corey navigated the rocks to sit next to Daniel, slipping into his usual place. "Then I won't."

"Is everyone still here?" Daniel asked. "It's late. What about Sophie's school?"

"I took them back, but you weren't in the kitchen, and Sophie missed her cookies, so I decided to come back for them and for you," he bumped elbows. "Actually it was more for you. I was worried."

"I told you I have these times when I get weird and I need to be alone."

Corey tipped his head back to look at the stars, and Daniel followed suit. Otherwise he would stare at Corey.

Corey began to talk. "I want to say we can forget everything that happened, how our stories connected and why we met. I know we can't, but I want to learn more about you, like what happened today? Was it talking to Gabriel? Or was it something I did? Did I take the kiss too far and spook you?" Corey took his hand and laced their fingers. "I'm sorry if it was me. I'm a bull in a china shop."

"I wanted that kiss as much as you did."

"Then I'm glad for that."

Indecision warred with the need to be honest. Gabriel was right. Everyone had an origin story, a reason why they became the person they were. Was it the kind of parents a child was born to? Or was it genetics that mixed in to make a man good? What if a child had no parents, and genetics never had a chance to shape them properly? What if a child was snatched from the side of the road and forced to a place where they were hurt all the time?

*What kind of story is* my *story?*

"Frank was a minister," Daniel began in a small voice. "Father Frank Martins, and he was driving home with his daughter Andrea. They looked alike, and she had a lovely smile, and I trusted them. I was fourteen, and I was on the road because I'd skipped out on yet another foster home, and my buddy hadn't come back to get me where he'd left me. I decided to walk. Only I was lost, it was dark, and I was a kid. I was scared. This truck stopped and the driver said he'd take me into Laredo, and what kind of minister with his daughter was going to hurt a kid? Right?"

Corey gripped his hand tight and made a small noise of distress as if he knew from the start how this story ended.

Daniel cleared his throat. "So he drops his daughter at home and says he'll take me the last few miles into the city, to the bus station, to a phone, to call someone. Anyone. He gave me a bottle of water, and I drank it, and I think it was drugged." He paused. "No, I *know* it was drugged. I slept. When I woke up, I was in a room no window, a bed like you see in jails, a mattress, that was it. By the time I ended up being rescued, I'd been there too long. Two years. I was hard and had a shield around me, but I stood up in court with Kyle, Gabriel, and Liam, and I put the two men I knew away."

"Hank and Yuri."

"Yep. They got theirs. Yuri was knifed soon after, right in the gut, found the next morning in his cell. Justice. And Hank, he's still locked up, but he's playing games, says he's ill." Daniel tapped his head. "It's us that were damaged mentally, not him." He briefly squeezed Corey's hand and then sighed and relaxed into him.

Corey disentangled their fingers and instead put his arm around Daniel's shoulder and pulled him close, kissing the top of his head and resting his chin there.

"What about Frank?" Corey asked after a short pause.

"Dead. Killed himself when Hank and Yuri were

arrested. I handed over his name to the cops, but our lawyer told me Frank had committed suicide. He showed me a newspaper. Frank had been involved in child abuse, that was what the papers said, but his story died soon after. No one on our case was interested in a minister who had disgraced himself. Apparently, he'd gotten his punishment. It's wrong in God's eyes to take your own life. There's a picture of his funeral online. His obituary said he left a wife and daughter, but his daughter wasn't at the funeral."

"You think she knew what her dad was doing?"

Some memory flashed in his head, a glimpse of something he thought was her in his recurring dreams. "I have no idea. I don't care." He stopped as soon as he said that because the truth was, he *did* care. It was something that had poked at him for a long time. What if she had known and was possibly doing the same thing herself now? She'd been a girl, but was she like her dad? What if she had her own children? When he recalled some of the things Frank had done to him and imagined it happening to kids like the one he once was, it made him feel sick.

"So that's my origin story," he finished and smiled, aware that Corey wouldn't get the reference at all. It hadn't been as hard to tell someone as he thought, but that was probably because Corey wasn't just *someone*.

"It's hard to hear, but I'm glad you trust me to tell me," Corey murmured. Then they sat in silence.

The night was warm, the stars bright, and tucked into Corey's side, Daniel began to relax. Telling Corey hadn't been as terrifying as he thought it would be. If anything, it was a relief to get everything out in the open. He didn't judge Daniel for getting in the car or for who he trusted or the fact he didn't want to think about Frank's daughter, Andrea, or what was happening to her now.

Now he was thinking about kissing Corey, and wanting Corey, and wondering if perhaps they could move this on now?

"Can I kiss you?" he asked, twisting out of Corey's support and moving lithely to straddle his lap, which was awkward and laughable if Corey didn't immediately get with the program and kiss him. He wriggled to get comfortable, taking the weight off Corey, and then deepened the kiss. The slide of their tongues was the most erotic thing he'd ever done, and he was hard.

"My turn to ask," Corey said when they separated to breathe. "Please let me touch you?" His hands were on Daniel's lower back, and when Daniel nodded, they slid under his shirt, and they were cold. Daniel hissed at the contact and then realized the coolness was nice against his skin, and he wanted Corey's hands inside his jeans. It seemed that Corey had the same idea, and between kisses and seeking reassurances that Daniel was okay with this, Corey unbuttoned his fly and closed his fingers around Daniel's cock.

Daniel pressed into the hold, grinding himself against Corey's hand, and the kisses grew frantic. Had he ever come like this before? Had he ever felt this way? He'd spent so much time questioning whether what happened to him had broken him and wondering if he would ever feel anything for a man again.

Corey moved what little he could but mostly allowed Daniel to direct what was happening, and Daniel had to consciously try and slow himself down, so close to coming just from this touch. He didn't want that.

*This has to be done right.*

Whatever that meant. He only knew that he wanted Corey to come at the same time, wanted desperately for this to be good for him as well.

"Help me," he demanded and tried to get between them to get his hands on Corey, but Corey shook his head, concentrating hard on Daniel.

"Let me do it."

Abruptly it was done. Daniel fucking into Corey's hand and coming so hard he closed his eyes and buried his face in Corey's neck. He stayed there, Corey still moving beneath him, breathing harshly, and then cursing in Daniel's ear as he came, and finally went still.

Corey was the first to talk, although it was more of a chuckle.

"I'm falling in love with you," he said in a tone that implied it was something totally, beautifully, unexpected.

*I already have. Don't hurt me. Don't leave me.*

Daniel kissed Corey's neck, then kissed a path to his lips. Could he be brave enough to say what he was feeling, to share the things that were in his heart?

"I love you too," he whispered to the wide-open sky and secretive night.

And to Corey.

---

The dream caught him in the dark. The same woman calling to him, telling him it was all okay when it clearly wasn't. Her hair remained over her face, a veil he couldn't see through, but the way she held herself? Memories assailed him, and he clung to them even as the dream became a nightmare.

He woke sobbing in Corey's hold.

And Corey didn't let him go until he was calm.

"Don't let me go," Daniel pleaded.

"Never," Corey said. "I promise."

## Chapter Fourteen

BEING IN LOVE MEANT THINKING ABOUT DANIEL AT THE weirdest times. Like in the shower or right now, when he was whipping up homemade mac 'n' cheese, his mom's recipe, for everyone on Wednesday night. Daniel didn't have a cellphone, so there was no way to just send him a text with a smiley face or check in on what he had for his dinner.

So much of Corey's life was wrapped up in being able to communicate fast and effectively, that he felt as if he'd lost a limb.

He was in love, and he wanted to post about it on his Instagram or update his Facebook profile or *anything* so that other people knew how he was feeling. Maybe he should get Daniel to have a cell or at the very least some kind of social network presence. Then perhaps he could stop reaching for his phone to tell Daniel something only to realize he couldn't.

"Have you thought about phoning him at Legacy?"

Amy helpfully suggested when he complained about this lack of channels to connect with Daniel.

*Shit.* Calling him on a landline phone had never even crossed his mind.

But what if the phone was emergency use only? What if, when he was blowing up the line talking about Daniel's day, some kid in the city was trying to connect to Legacy?

Amy thought that was probably the case, so the idea was shelved.

Which still left him itchy and lost and needing to connect with Daniel.

Sophie was the one who made sense of it all.

"If he's going to be your best friend, you should go play at his place," she offered with all her young-kid logic. "Same as when I go and play at Milly's house."

He opened his mouth to explain it wasn't the same thing, and then it hit him. Why wasn't he just getting in the car and driving over to Legacy? He pulled Sophie into a hug, and she wriggled away and wiped at her face where he'd planted a patented big brother kiss.

"Ewww," she muttered and then went back to coloring.

"Amy?"

Amy peered up from her book, some thick tome on molecular biology that had her fascinated.

"What?" she blinked away the unfocused look in her eyes, then glanced at the dinner Corey was preparing. "Is it ready?"

"Will you take over? Are you in tonight?"

She eyed him suspiciously. "Yeah?"

He washed his hands. "I'm going to Legacy."

This time the suspicion morphed into something he recognized. A sibling recognizing an opening for teasing.

"Daniel will love that," she singsonged, and he gave her the finger.

"That's rude," Sophie admonished.

He made a show of hiding the offending finger. "My bad," he said, then ruffled her hair. "Food, finish your homework, bed, Amy's in charge."

Sophie sighed dramatically. "One day I will be in charge."

Amy hugged her from behind. "Only if we get a dog."

"Are we getting a dog?" Sophie asked, twisting in Amy's hold. "Corey, are we getting a dog?"

Corey backed out of the kitchen slowly. "Talk to Amy," he shouted as he left.

Traffic was light, and by seven he was pulling into Legacy. When he knocked on the door, Kyle opened it, and he went from welcoming to alert in a second.

"What is it? Is it one of the girls? What happened?"

"Nothing." Corey held up a hand. "I'm here to see Daniel."

There was movement behind Kyle, and then he was unceremoniously shoved to one side, and there was Daniel, as confused as Kyle had been a few moments earlier.

Corey didn't give Daniel time to think. He grasped his hand and tugged him out of the door. Daniel went with him quietly until they reached the barn, and finally, he eased his hand out of Corey's.

"What's wrong?" he asked.

Corey kissed him, hard, soft, then hard again, pushing him back until he hit the barn wall and then twisting them, so it was him who was trapped against the wood. He tangled his hands in Daniel's hair and kissed him with every particle of feeling in his body. The kiss was wild and unstructured until abruptly it slowed and became something more.

Daniel rested a hand on the wall, and with the other, he cupped Corey's cheek, looking into his eyes and then smiled.

"Are you okay?" he asked. As if there was some dire reason why Corey was here to see him.

"I'm fine, I…" he kissed Daniel again, and he wanted to get closer, to kiss Daniel all night if he could. "I love you," he said between kisses. "I want to kiss you all the time."

Daniel didn't argue, but the kisses changed, less desperate and more searching, with soft words that no one else could hear. They only parted when Daniel's stomach rumbled.

"I hadn't even got to eat dinner," he complained.

Still, it was another fifteen minutes before they went inside.

---

Life moved treacle-slow, from weekend to weekend, broken only by short visits to Legacy during the week when missing Daniel became too much to handle. Corey had cleared the last of the paperwork from Dryden-Marsdale, everything in the house scanned, logged, and now in the hands of the courier that the new manifestation of the company had booked. Handing over that last box had been both soul-destroying and freeing.

He was done with it, and now he didn't know what to do.

Closing the massive front door, he then turned and

leaned back on it, looking up at the mini chandelier that hung there. His mom had been so proud of that, overseeing its four-times-a-year cleaning as diligently as she'd taken care of the rest of the house. She hated that she couldn't do the chandelier herself, but his stubborn, smart mom couldn't do *everything*. Or at least that was what Dad used to say.

Thoughts of his parents were always there. Sometimes he forgot they were gone, and when he remembered, it was as if he had to restart the grieving process all over again. He wondered about things. What they would think of Daniel.? Would they have approved of him and the girls selling their stakes in Dryden-Marsdale? Did they want the siblings to stay in the house or move on? Were they proud of how their children were coping?

"Is that done?" Chloe asked from the stairs, scaring the shit out of him.

He shot a foot in the air and clutched at his chest. "Jesus, Chloe," he snapped and then asked the standard question, "How long have you been sitting there?"

"I heard the knock on the door, is all."

She was quiet, a little sad, and he moved to sit next to her on the step she was on, which was level with the top of the chandelier. He could see the dust that stopped the crystals from glowing and knew he needed to add a clean to his mental to-do list. Mom would be pissed if her beautiful possessions were left to deteriorate.

He bumped shoulders with Chloe and then leaned back on his elbows.

"Yeah, that was the last of the papers from Dad's office."

"What will you do now? For work I mean?"

Corey didn't need to work, not for a long time. There was enough money in the pot to keep the house running for his sisters and to enable him to pick and choose what he did next. He had planned on studying more, to become better at that, to teach other people, maybe. Then there was the writing. Taking over after Dad died had been expected but not welcomed at all.

"I don't know. What about you?" He knew she'd been to see that guy in the city, Jack and Riley's friend Steve, about possible placements, but she'd been asleep by the time he'd gotten back from seeing Daniel the night before, so this was the first time he'd been able to catch up.

"Steve is cool. He's super rich, you know, like obscenely rich?"

"What the hell? He told you that?" *What kind of man tells an impressionable young girl he's super rich?* Corey's defenses rose immediately, and he tensed, ready to grab his keys and go talk to Steve, wherever he was.

"No," she poked him, "you wouldn't know it. He wears a suit but never a tie, and his wife was there in the meeting, and she's super cute. I looked him up though. He's on this top one hundred Texas list for what he's worth."

"Oh." Corey relaxed a little. Riley and Jack were likely on that list as well, and they were good guys. Even so, he resolved to meet up with Steve, as the responsible guardian he was.

"So, Steve offered me an internship, and I thought I'd take my money from the sale and maybe buy a small place near the office. In a safe apartment block," she added quickly, probably aware that Corey was going to have something to say about that. She'd turned eighteen a month or so back, but that didn't make her grown up.

"You're eighteen." he wanted desperately to put the word "only" in that summation.

"Mom was eighteen when she left home and met Dad."

Corey couldn't argue with that. He wanted to say times were different, and that made him feel so damn old. Instead, he channeled what he hoped his mom and dad would say.

"That's good," he began. "I'd want you to let me be involved in finding a place, vetting it, and you'd have to agree to come home at least twice a week for dinner, just so Sophie can see you." He ran out of words then as she reached for his hand and laced their fingers.

"Family is the priority," she murmured. "But it's also time for me to do what I need to do."

Just like Amy who was going onto further education, and Sophie who was ruling the roost in her grade, Chloe was making a path for herself.

"Okay." He wondered if it even mattered what her big brother wanted or said.

"It does," she said.

"What?" He looked at her.

"You said did it matter what my big brother wants."

"I said that out loud?"

"Yep, and yes, we make decisions together. You know I was thinking about things." She stopped and then turned more on the stair. "What are we doing with the house?"

"I don't know. I thought we should stay until Sophie's old enough to decide for herself. It's not like her holding in Dryden; it's the heart of our family at the moment."

She relaxed then. "Agreed. But let's think about moving on, okay? I don't want to be here."

"Really?"

"No, it feels wrong now, but also I want to do what is right for Sophie." She sighed softly and leaned back. Decisions about selling the house would be for another day.

They both stared at the ceiling.

"I should get someone in to clean the chandelier," he commented to her, in a way so that she knew it was on his to-do list. "Mom would kill us if we let it go to ruin."

She laughed. "Do you remember last time when the cleaner dropped one of the crystals, and Mom chased him out of the house?"

Corey grinned at that. He hadn't been there, but the image of his mom telling the experienced craftsman to get out of the house was so like her. She was a strong, determined woman.

"You have a lot of Mom in you."

Chloe squeezed his hand. "Thank you."

Corey needed to pull up a memory that wasn't so hard to bear.

"Do you remember when we had the tent fort and Mom was determined to get in with us, and she was in this dress with the sequins, ready for some ball that she was going to with Dad?" he asked.

"Oh my god, yeah."

"And she got stuck on the grate in the floor and lost an earring down the grill."

Chloe snorted with laughter. "And she lay there laughing like an idiot, telling Dad to go without her, and he had to climb in, all dressed up himself to release her."

"He ended up lying in there with us, and they were late. I remember that."

"She was pregnant, I think, with Sophie?"

Corey let the discussion wash over him, remembering that night and the laughter, and when Chloe went upstairs, Corey went to the office and sat in his dad's chair.

Built in the early nineteen hundreds, the sprawling Edwardian had a whole series of grates and ducts that had once delivered heat around the house. Of course, the place had central heating now, and the ducts were primarily covered up, all apart from one in the kitchen under the pan drawer and the one in the office.

*Maybe the earring is still there?*

He crouched by the grate, using his cell phone to check inside. It was doubtful his mom's earring was still in there, after all. He remembered the pair had glittered brightly, so he assumed they were diamonds. Reflective material caught the light though, but he couldn't quite make out what it was, so he sat back on his heels and looked for something to pry it open with. There wasn't much left in there, but he saw the old letter opener with the onyx handle and dull blade, and that was enough to clear the dust from the sides and get some traction on the grate.

He lifted it carefully and then directed his phone into the space. The metal was a paperclip, and he saw there was more, what seemed like one of his dad's journals, and he knew that this had to be the missing journal from four years ago. It wasn't easy to get out. It was as if his dad had wedged it deep, and it only just came through the opening, and that was at an angle. By the time he had the book, his hand had been scraped raw.

Why was there a journal so hidden away that it might

never be found? Surely one day they would leave this house, and a new owner would find it? What was so important it had to be hidden? Then, he thought his dad would have imagined he'd be back to take it out.

*He'd never planned on dying.*

He scooted back to rest against the leg of the desk and checked out what he'd found. As he thought, it was the missing journal, dated September, but there was no end date on it like the others. It had loose pages shoved inside, and he was scared to open it. In his heart, he knew what was in there. The PI investigation had begun soon after that date, and this could be his dad finding out what kind of brother he had, wrestling with what to do about it. He pulled out the loose pages. They were dated more recently, and he put them to one side.

The entries were a jumbled mess of thoughts, and there was an entire page detailing why he couldn't leave the journal with the others. How Corey's mom had a key to them, and she didn't know anything about the kind of man Drake was. Dad had detailed that he'd found the other boys, and Daniel, and that he'd set up a foundation to give Daniel a scholarship, taking over from the Campbell-Hayes who had an anonymous fund in place for Daniel. That one day he wanted to meet Jack and Riley specifically to talk about their Legacy Ranch.

By the time he'd finished reading the journal, and worse, the extra notes, his world had turned inside out, but he knew two things.

He had to tell Daniel and the others.

And, then, maybe it was time to tell the world.

He didn't know how to do this. So he went straight to the only man who wasn't on the D or Legacy right now, and probably the only person who could pull everything together without making a mess of things. He didn't have an appointment, but when he arrived at CH Consulting to visit with Riley, he wasn't turned away. The receptionist was nothing but courteous.

When he apologized for the lack of an appointment but that he really needed to talk to Riley and asked if he was in, she sat him down in a small alcove with coffee and made a call. Evidently, Riley wasn't here at the office, and would he mind waiting for a short while? She kept glancing at him, as the clock ticked on fifteen minutes, then thirty. At least she wasn't throwing him out, and he wasn't moving.

How long he sat there, he didn't know, but when a steady hand cupped his shoulder, he was startled out of his thoughts as he looked up into hazel eyes.

"Corey," Riley said. "You want to come with me?"

Corey followed him, staring at his back in a daze, clutching the journal to his chest and wondering how the hell he was going to explain this.

There was more coffee, and a long silence, in this room with blinds and a coffee machine, and what appeared to be a cot. He focused on the green cupboards on the wall and the lamp on the ceiling. This must've been some kind of medical room or something.

Riley finally broke the silence. "Jack would have come as well, but he's at Legacy this morning, and I was in meetings in the city."

"It's okay. One of you is fine." God, that sounded rude,

and he wanted to apologize, but the words stuck in his throat.

Riley sat forward in his seat, serious expression in place, and Corey met his gaze.

"I found my dad's journal from the time he found out that Drake was abusing kids, and like we now know, that he'd paid to go to this place called Bar Five."

"Okay?"

"Drake was being blackmailed by some asshole who ran poker games, which is why he took money from the business. My dad paid them the rest of what Drake owed, made him vow to turn over a new leaf, said he wouldn't prosecute. He never asked what Drake was being blackmailed for, but then he asked a PI to dig further, and it all came out. Every sordid detail. It's all in here." He clutched the journal even harder, his fingers numb. "There were photos, and Dad wrote that his brother was *wrong in the head.* The rest? I don't know everything, but there are loose pages taken from later journals, and every one of them details building a profile of my uncle."

Riley listened as the information flooded out of Corey. "Did your dad tell anyone else? The cops?"

Corey nodded. "A DA in Denver, a friend of his from when he was at college. I spoke to him, and he told me this, which explains why they were…" He bowed his head. *Why they were flying to Denver. Why he'd used a stupid flimsy excuse to get Drake in the plane with them. Why they'd been arguing because his dad was taking Drake to hand him over to the DA. Why his mom was on the flight as someone who could keep the two men calm.* Everything.

"What else is there?"

"He tried to track down every single person he thought

was hurt by Drake. There are details in there about each one of you. The arrivals at Legacy, the work you and Jack do, the kind of men you were. But he was too late to help any of you. Except for Daniel. He set up a trust for Daniel's education, one that replaced what Jack had set up for him I think."

Riley didn't look surprised at the news his husband had been funding Daniel's education. "Sounds right," he murmured.

"Dad wanted it to be something he could do without Daniel knowing it was from him."

"Okay," Riley said. "We should think about what you're going to do next."

"I know what I have to do. I need to give this to someone who can work out what to do with the information. I don't want it. My sisters need to know about Drake, I can't keep it from them anymore. But, we won't know what to do with it all."

All he could think of was Daniel and what his family had done to him. How his uncle had been part of something so heinous that it defied explanation. What was in here could destroy the progress Daniel had made in his life so far.

"Come on. Let's do what I always do when I can't get my head around something." Riley stood. "Ask Jack. he'll know what to do."

## Chapter Fifteen

DANIEL WASN'T EXACTLY HIDING, BUT HE *WAS* ENJOYING the coffee and cookie and his quiet time with Hennessy, who kept nudging at his arm, wanting attention.

"Thought you'd be in here." Jason took a seat on the low garden wall next to him. "Kyle wants to talk to you."

"Now?" This was supposed to be his quiet time, and he treasured it, away from the general confusion of the ranch. He loved the garden that Corey and his sisters had worked so hard on. Checking out the next crop ready for harvesting and the green against the dark wood of a trellis with peas climbing skyward was beautiful. A garden was peace, and one day he'd like to see the rose garden at Corey's place; the one he talked about a lot.

He felt as if he could do that soon, spend a night away from Legacy. Maybe even stay in Corey's bed, take things to the next level, possibly.

"Are you even listening to me?" Jason teased and stole the cookie from where it sat on Daniel's knee. Daniel tried to get it, back and they tussled like idiots for a few moments before Jason stuffed the whole lot into his mouth, ending up the image of a demented hamster.

"You're an asshole," Daniel said, but there was no heat there.

Jason started to speak, but the cookie made it impossible, which was a win. Daniel stood, brushed off crumbs, and headed for the house but not before cuffing Jason around the back of the head and watching bits of cookie fly out of his mouth.

When he walked into the kitchen, he knew something was wrong. Not at first. His first instinct was to be happy because Corey was here, and he crossed over to kiss him, but the kiss he got in return was quiet and a little desperate, Corey clinging to him for just a few seconds longer than Daniel expected. It was after the kiss that he realized Kyle, Liam, and Jack sat at the large round table, and Gabriel was there as well, along with Riley.

Riley stood by the sink, his hands pushed into his pockets. And everyone appeared so damned serious that Daniel's stomach fell. Was this an intervention or a complaint? Was he being asked to go? He thought he'd been doing okay. What had he done to fuck it up?

"I don't want to go," Daniel said, not caring if he sounded needy and pathetic. This was his home. He had a room here; Jack said so. "You can't make me. Please."

"What?" Kyle asked, looking up from a book in front of him.

"No one is making anyone go," Jack said with feeling.

"This is just a meeting," Riley pointed out.

"We're leaving," Jack said, "but guys, whatever you decide, honesty is vital here. Get everything out in the open, and then, whatever you decide, we'll have your backs. Whether you draw a line under it or decide to push for more justice."

They all waited for Jack and Riley to leave. Then Daniel couldn't wait a moment longer.

"What does Jack mean by justice?" He checked each person in turn. Gabriel was edgy, wouldn't meet his gaze. On the other hand, Liam stared right at him, stoic and thin-lipped. Then there was Kyle, who had an expression that suggested someone had killed his horse. "What kind of a meeting is this?"

"I found something of my dad's," Corey explained at his side. Hell, he'd forgotten Corey was here for a moment. "That pertains to your case."

Typically, Daniel loved it when Corey used words like *pertain*, kissing the syllables from his lips, but right now he wasn't seeing Corey-who-loved-him standing here.

"We need to vote after you've seen this," Kyle said and pushed the paperwork to a place in front of an empty chair. Daniel guessed that was where he was supposed to sit and took the chair, fear curling inside him. What had happened?

He pulled the book toward him, a simple green journal, with a date in permanent black ink on the front. It said *September,* and there was a hyphen implying there would be an end date, but the space where it would have gone was empty.

"It's my dad's," Corey explained and sat in the chair opposite him.

"You told me there were journals," Daniel said immediately. "Why did you only bring one of them?"

Gabriel jumped on that. "Wait. There's more of this crap?"

Corey shook his head. "No, the others are just family life. Sophie losing a tooth, me getting my degree, the weather, the garden. Just thoughts."

Gabriel subsided with a muttered curse and then stared at his hands. "Shoulda brought Cam," he complained.

"Corey?" Daniel asked and waited for Corey to look at him, giving him a small smile. Corey smiled back, but it didn't reach his eyes. He seemed as if he wanted to cry.

So Daniel did the only thing he could. He opened the journal and began to read. The entries were done every day at the start. Simple things like the fact Corey had won an award for English, and how proud his dad was of him. Then the entries grew a little darker, spoke about anonymous information regarding Drake Dryden. How he didn't want to believe what the letter he'd received said, but he had doubts about his own brother. There were details of adoption records, a sketched family tree, and the day that he decided to hire a PI to track Drake's stealing of money and possible mistreating of children and young adults.

The journal missed some days after that, and Daniel didn't have to be a genius to assume that Corey's father didn't know what to write when the weight of his brother's possible guilt was dragging him down. Then the entries stopped abruptly. He flicked the pages, and then, when he saw nothing at all, he turned to the loose leaves.

Details of everything Drake Dryden had done. Specific dates and times of car journeys, money stolen to cover being blackmailed, and worst of all, Daniel's address at college under his real name. He never thought he'd be able to hide who he was, that wasn't the intention, but the money he'd been given from the sale of the Bar

Five had helped him start a new life for himself as Daniel Brown.

Then there was a detailed account of the money that had formed Daniel's scholarship, from Jack, and then from Corey's dad.

Next to Daniel's name, a code of sorts that he didn't recognize, and finally, there was a letter, dated September four years back. It was a long letter, passionately written by someone saying they knew things that needed to be told.

*Andrea. The girl from the truck. The minister's daughter.*

The last paragraph he read again after it didn't make sense the first time.

*The monster I called Dad was responsible for picking up at least one of the boys. I know because I was in the car. I remember he was named Daniel and that he was about my age, fourteen or so, maybe fifteen. I didn't know what Frank Martins was. I don't know if my mother did, but to me, he was just Dad and a man of God. I told him what I knew, said I was telling the authorities, and he shook his head as if I'd disappointed him. That was the last time I saw him alive. He killed himself soon after, and I hope for one that the God that he talks about so much in the pulpit judges him for what he's done and that he burns in hell.*

The letter was signed with a simple *Andrea*, but her address was below it, and a number.

Carefully, Daniel folded the letter, pushed it into his pocket.

"That's evidence," Corey said, his words broken. "Part of the whole story."

"Not your story," Daniel said. "My story." He looked

at the three others who had suffered alongside him. "Our story." He wasn't angry or defensive. The words were simple, and that was the end of the discussion.

"I can't imagine what you're feeling." Corey was devastated. Daniel could tell from the way he said that, and then stared down at the table. A large part of him wanted to reassure Corey that everything was going to be okay. But the call to deal with what he'd read and to leave the kitchen and stand in the dark, was overwhelming. He even stood up, but then just as quickly he sat. He didn't need to run to work through his feelings. He could stay right here with the rest of them. It was Corey who should leave.

It seemed as if Corey got the silent message, and he let himself out of the kitchen. "I'll be outside if you need me." Only when he was gone did the meeting of the four of them begin.

"First off, Daniel, are you okay?" Liam asked, his hands knotted together on the table in front of him.

There were so many ways to answer that. All he could think was, *why are you even asking me that?*

"Are you?" he asked Liam in return, feeling guilty when he shook his head.

"Do we take this to the cops?" Gabriel asked.

Kyle cleared his throat. "For me, it's done. I'm pissed. No, more than pissed, but this Drake guy is dead. We've already stood up in court and told them everything we could. There's no one else left alive to punish, and it serves no purpose to drag it all up again." He paused and closed his eyes momentarily. "But this isn't all about me."

Gabriel chewed on his lip and then scrubbed his eyes. "Look, I want to say that I'd love everyone to know the names, to see what damage was done. But, no. I agree we should draw a line under it. I think we've all suffered enough with this," Gabriel said. "What is the point in dragging this on for longer. Who will it help?"

Liam nodded, and all of them looked at Daniel. What did they want him to say?

"Gabriel, you said we should own our origin stories." He stood, and Gabriel followed the action.

"What are you doing?"

"I'll come back, I promise."

"Don't leave. We need to talk about this," Gabriel said urgently.

Kyle moved between him and Daniel and placed a hand on Gabriel's chest. "Let him go, Gabriel. He needs to make decisions for himself before we can all make one together. Give Daniel time."

Daniel walked backward until he hit the door. Liam had his eyes closed, Gabriel appeared as if he wanted to drag Daniel back, but Kyle? He was at peace. Anyone could see that.

"I just need a minute," Daniel reassured, talking more to Gabriel than anyone else. "Please, trust me."

He slid out of the door and spotted Corey outside, leaning against his car, staring down at his phone. The light illuminated his face, and he was as broken as Gabriel had been. Daniel pulled out the paper and stalked over, Corey looking up at the sound of his footsteps and straightening.

"Daniel—"

"Can you give me your phone?"

Corey blinked at him, looked shocked and unfocused, and then seemed to pull himself together and handed it over, and Daniel checked it out, then handed it right back.

"This is the number." He thrust out the paper.

"Andre? This might not have that number anymore," Corey said, even as he dialed, but then there was ringing, and a female answered the phone. Daniel took the handset and put it to his ear.

"Hello?" the woman asked.

"Is this Andrea?" Daniel asked with every ounce of strength he possessed to keep the tone even. The last time he'd seen this woman was when she'd been a girl, and she'd smiled at him so prettily.

As if he'd meant something in her world. As if he was a real human being whose existence mattered, not just a foster family's burden.

She'd been beautiful. He wondered if she still was.

"Who is this?" she asked after some moments. She evidently wasn't going to tell him her name, and who could blame her. She'd seen the hateful dark side of humanity. Hell, he was surprised she'd even answered her phone.

"This is Daniel," he said coolly, calmly.

There were some sounds, rustling, the noise of a door shutting, and then she was back on the line, her voice echoing. "Who?"

"I'm Daniel Brown now, but I *was* Daniel Chandler."

She made a noise then, like a wounded animal, a cry of disbelief and despair, and he waited for her to say something next.

"I'm sorry," she said. "So sorry, for what happened. I didn't know what kind of man he was. I didn't know what he'd done."

Corey took his free hand, his expression one of concern and love, and Daniel gripped it tightly.

"I know you didn't." Daniel wasn't lying. "No one knew what those men did."

She began to cry, trying to stop herself. "I'm so sorry. Can you ever forgive me?"

There was a noise of a door opening.

"Andrea baby, Lyle says he needs a cuddle."

"Not now, Mark. I'm… can you …?" She was clearly telling whoever this *Mark* was, to go, but it seemed as if he was a stubborn asshole who refused to listen.

"Who is this?" he demanded, apparently having taken the phone from her.

"Daniel Chandler," Daniel said with conviction in his tone.

"Shit," the man cursed, and then he sighed. "I'm putting you on the loudspeaker. We're in the garage. Keep talking, but I'm warning you, I'm recording this if you want to threaten us."

Keep talking? He had nothing else to say other than he didn't blame Andrea for the time he was kept on the Bar Five.

Because it was done. She was in pain as well as him. Not the same maybe, but she'd learned her dad was a monster and lost him all in the same short space of time. She had to live with that.

"I need to ask Andrea a question, but I understand if you don't want me to."

There was silence, and then Andrea spoke, her voice shaky. "I'm listening."

Daniel closed his eyes briefly. "I see you in my dreams, all the time. Not from when I got in that car, never from that, but you are older. Why are you in my dreams?"

Mark made a noise. "How can she answer that?"

He and Andrea had a low conversation, and Daniel let them talk. Finally, she began again.

"What is it I do in your dreams?"

"You help me; you get me away from there. Is that what you did?"

Mark intervened again. "Don't say anything that could incriminate you."

"For god's sake, Mark, what can anyone do to us now? They're all dead. Daniel? Are you still there?"

"I'm here."

"I didn't know what kind of evil he was, not until I found some photos on his laptop, and abruptly things fell in place. Some of the whispers I'd heard, some of the things I'd seen. Him working away, picking you up in our car, and then not coming home. He said he was doing God's work in the city, but I knew something was wrong. I followed him, found the ranch, couldn't do anything, and then Mark helped me."

There was a more heated debate between Mark and Andrea, but most of it was muffled, her hand over the receiver, he thought. Then Andrea was back.

"Mark and I sneaked in, found you, got you away, and then called the cops. When I got home, I told my father what I'd found, and he left then. When we found him dead, he'd committed suicide, and I felt nothing. Just that I'd helped to destroy you, and any others my dad had hurt. I gave everything to the local cops, all the data, the names, the addresses, the photos. They handed it up, and there was the trial for the two ringleaders. But my dad was a coward, he was dead. It was because of what I found out that things were in the light, but the trial? That was you, and the brave men who stood with you."

Daniel felt a hundred emotions all warring for dominance, and then he realized all he felt was apathy. As if he was listening to someone else's story. Not his.

"I don't have anything else to say," Daniel offered.

"I don't expect you to say a thing. I tried to make things right, and Mark was there for me. I wanted you to have someone for yourself."

He leaned into Corey. "I do, now. Who is Lyle?"

"Our son," Andrea said, not calling him on the change of direction.

"Andrea, I want you to know, you say you wanted to ask me to forgive you, but there is nothing to forgive. Neither of us knew what he was. Maybe we hurt differently, but in our hearts maybe it's the same."

"How can you say that after what happened to you?" she asked, and she was crying again.

Daniel sighed. "Mark, are you there still?"

Mark's voice was a little less strident this time. Actually, he sounded more cautious. "I am."

"I'm not revisiting this because I won't let it hurt me anymore. Mark, I need you to hug Andrea and tell her I don't need to forgive her, but I will if it makes her feel better. Because no one deserves the ghost of what Frank did ruling their lives. I'm going now. I have friends I need to reassure."

"Thank you, Daniel," Andrea said. He went to end the call but heard her cautious "could we maybe meet up one day?"

Daniel shook his head and then realized she wouldn't see that. "No." He softened his tone. "That's not part of my story, Andrea. Thank you, enjoy Mark and your son, be happy."

He ended the call before either Andrea or Mark could say anything else, not giving them a chance to reopen old wounds or crack the determination he had to keep the past in the past.

What was the point in going back there? He'd had counseling, he'd dealt with most things, Legacy was healing him, and he was in love. That was his future. Legacy and Corey were his future.

Corey kissed him gently on the forehead, then held him close until Daniel eased away.

Hand in hand they went back into the kitchen, and all three men turned to face them.

"I want to burn it all," Daniel announced. "I don't want it to touch my life again." He looked at Corey. "Is that okay? These are your dad's words."

"I don't want it," Corey said. "The girls won't want it."

Gabriel was the first to reach him, hugging him, and Kyle was the one who picked up the papers and stood by the door. Liam was slower but only because he wanted to hug Daniel as well and Gabriel wasn't letting him go.

Daniel held out a hand for Corey to come with them, but he shook his head and sat in the kitchen. Daniel knew that was for the best; he guessed this part of the story was just for the four men of Bar Five. They stood over the fire pit that Jason and Gabriel had created only a few weeks ago, and Kyle lit a fire.

This information could all be found again if anyone cared to look but symbolically what they had here needed to be burned.

Liam went first, ripped out a whole bunch of pages and tossed them in without words. Then he doubled over as if pain had knifed in his belly, and Gabriel held him up when it looked like he was crying. Curiously, Kyle remained the calmest, taking more of the pages and throwing them into the orange flames.

"Done," he announced, then crossed his arms over his chest in defiance at any demons who might have raised themselves from the notes.

Gabriel took the remainder of the journal and took his time burning it all, watching thin-lipped and silent as single pages curled and blackened.

Then it was Daniel's turn. He took the loose pages of information and held them over the heat, wincing when it grew too hot on his hand. Kyle placed a hand on his shoulder.

"Let go, Daniel."

The papers fell, some sliding sideways in the updraft, others destroyed on impact. Soon everything was gone, and all four of them stood back and stared at the flames.

"Wait here," Kyle said, going indoors and then bringing out a selection of beer and water. Each of them took a drink.

"To us." Kyle raised his water.

"Always," Liam said.

"To us," Gabriel repeated.

"To the future," Daniel offered. And he meant it.

## Chapter Sixteen

COREY WAITED FOR EVERYONE TO GET BACK INTO THE kitchen, knowing he'd stay right there until he could see Daniel. He agreed the papers should be burned, and the secret would die with them, but he was still plagued by the things he hadn't told his sisters.

The four men were out there symbolically destroying everything, but he still had what the PI had found, and he resolved to talk to Amy and Chloe about their uncle. He didn't want to be the keeper of the family's secrets, not with Daniel right in the middle of them. They had to know.

When the door opened, the scent of a bonfire filtered in with them, and he waited for whatever Daniel wanted to do next. Was he going to tell Corey to leave? Or stay? He had another letter in his pocket that was burning a hole there, and he wanted to explain to Corey why he'd kept it back, but face-to-face and alone.

Daniel held out a hand to him and tugged him out of the kitchen and into the smoky darkness, then past the fire pit and to his room. He unlocked the door and gestured for

Corey to go in first, locking the door behind them, then pushing a chair up and under the handle.

He stopped, then muttered something under his breath and removed the chair, leaving it to one side.

"I don't need that if you're here." He went straight into Corey's arms. Corey meant to show him the remaining letter. He certainly imagined that the minute they were alone, he would blurt out the rest of what he'd found.

Daniel didn't give him a chance.

They kissed and tumbled back onto Daniel's bed, Daniel sprawled over him kissing him with desperation. Something felt off, as if Daniel was forcing his feelings, and Corey wriggled out from under him and sat up.

"Wait," he said.

Daniel edged closer. "No waiting."

"There's something—"

Daniel cut off the words with another kiss, but this time it wasn't a kiss of desperation, but the sweetest, most careful kiss that Corey had ever been part of. All of his good intentions flew out of the window, and he ended up on his back again, but this time Daniel braced himself a little, and they kissed and moved until Daniel slipped between his spread legs. They were still dressed, only kissing, but this was an incredibly erotic experience. He was hard and could feel Daniel was the same, slipping his hands down Daniel's back and cupping his ass, pulling a little, and hearing the soft moan Daniel gave into the kiss.

"Too many clothes," Corey murmured, reaching between them and trying to unbutton Daniel's shirt.

With laughter and kisses, they managed to get shirts off, but at the last moment, Daniel clicked off the light, and they were plunged into darkness, the only illumination the ambient glow of the moon through the skylights. Corey wanted to turn the lamp back on, wanted to *see* Daniel, but he couldn't argue, not when Daniel was unbuttoning his jeans and finally had a hand on Corey's cock.

Corey scrabbled to touch Daniel, fighting the weight of him and the awkward angles until he'd managed to push Daniel's jeans down enough to *finally* get a hand on him as well. Desperation returned, but it was on both their sides, and with Daniel resting between Corey's legs, they rocked against each other and kissed until breathing became difficult. Whatever Daniel needed in this, Corey wanted him to have.

He'd do anything for Daniel.

Orgasm stole his breath, but he forced out Daniel's name, coming between them with Daniel not long after.

"I love you," Corey murmured.

Daniel smiled into a kiss and then buried his head in Corey's neck. "I love you too."

They stayed like that for the longest time when Daniel reached for the nearest thing, his shirt, and wiped the sticky mess they'd made. He tugged at the blankets and encouraged Corey to get under, then climbed in beside him and cuddled close. Corey tucked him under his arm and held him tightly. Nothing was pulling them apart. He was in love, Daniel loved him back, and there was nothing that could come between them.

*Tell him what else you found out.*

"Daniel?"

"Hmmm?"

"I found something else in the journal that I want you to know about."

For a moment Daniel was still, and then he sat up and

away and flicked on the lamp. Corey was bereft but knew this had to be done.

"What?" Daniel asked, and his tone was confrontational. He apparently expected the worst and was rightly angry that Corey would even bring something up that could ruin what had just happened.

"It's nothing bad." Corey prayed that the information wasn't actually a bad thing. Who knew? Daniel was fiercely defensive of what had happened to him. This was part of the story he'd spoken about, and Corey could prevaricate and work around the edges, introduce the subject slowly, and explain what he thought it meant, but he didn't. He ripped the Band-Aid off in one go.

"My mom and dad met at college in Denver, and my parents created the Legacy Foundation that funded a lot of scholarships there, including your last year scholarship with the express purpose of supporting you in what you were good at."

"I know, I read that."

"My dad kept an eye on you. Watched your progress."

Daniel's mouth fell open, and he crossed his arms over his chest, a defensive move, and to Corey, it was a barrier that came up. He was quiet, didn't react with words, or temper, or acceptance. He merely sat there, and Corey wanted to say something intelligent that would make this all right.

"You could have not told me that," Daniel said, his arms relaxing to his lap, and his voice firm.

Guilt flooded Corey. "I know. I thought about it, but you had to know." He moved closer to Daniel, held out a hand in entreaty. "What we have here is too special, too important, to have any secrets. I had to tell you. Not for me, but for us." Tears pricked at his eyes. He'd fucked this up.

Daniel considered the words. "I turned off the lamp," he said. But that made no sense at all. What was he saying? "Because I have scars on my back and some on my upper thigh, from *then*. I wasn't brave enough to let you see."

At first, Corey didn't see what that had to do with the scholarships, but then it hit him. They were being entirely honest here, getting all the hurt out.

"Can I see them?" he asked, not sure if Daniel would refuse. Instead, Daniel moved on the bed, so his back was to Corey, and for the first time, Corey saw the lines on Daniel's skin. They were faint, barely there, but they were marks he would carry forever. He touched one, ran the length of it, and Daniel shivered.

"There's more," Corey whispered. "My dad wrote that he'd seen your work at college, watched you run track, couldn't have been prouder of you if you were his own son. He wrote that you'd fought back, resumed your education, made it to college, and he saw something in you, passion and conviction. I have it to show you."

"Not tonight."

"No, but soon. He'd collected every report from your scholarship assessments, every piece of information in a small notebook. He hated that you were in any debt at all from college and has money in place to clear everything for you, but he died before he could tell you."

Daniel was thoughtful, his hands flat and relaxed on the bed beside him, and Corey could see every line of the man he loved. He wasn't moving away, or furious, or disappointed.

More importantly, he wasn't asking Corey to go, so Corey still had a chance to make things right.

"Talk to me," Corey pleaded.

"I have other things in my head. What your dad knew, how he helped me, how Jack helped me, that is a world away from me and you. None of what happened to me, or how people helped me, is your fault." Daniel tilted his head a little, his expression unreadable. "When I got in that car with Frank and his daughter, I had doubts. I ran them through my head, but I made the decision to get in the car."

"If you're going to tell me what happened to you was your fault..." He wasn't sure what he'd do if that was what Daniel was going to say next.

"What will you do if I do say that?" Daniel was intrigued.

Corey couldn't think, so he blurted out what came into his head first. "I'll tell you that you're wrong."

Daniel laughed then, a short, sharp burst, and he smiled. "I love you, Corey." He crawled toward him, easing him down until they were lying flat, then nudging the lamp with his toe. In the darkness, Corey clung to Daniel, wondering if maybe they were done talking.

But no. It seemed as if what Daniel had to say had to be told in the dark while holding tight to Corey.

"What your uncle did, what Frank did, none of that is on you, or me. What your parents might have discovered, and how they tried to fix it, that isn't on you either. I'm sorry if that is true, but it wasn't my fault."

"Of course it wasn't."

Daniel gripped Corey tighter, and they kissed. "I'll pay you and your sisters back," Daniel said, all serious.

"You don't have to. Shit, that was a scholarship you earned. Dad wrote that."

"It was a lot of money though. So Corey?"

"Uh-huh?"

"Now we're together, can I ask you a favor?"

"Anything."

"Any chance of borrowing the money to pay you back?"

The fucker was teasing him, and he was going to pay.

Laughter turned to tickling, which became far too heated to ignore. They made love again in the Texas moonlight, and all Corey could think was that in Daniel's arms he felt at peace. He just hoped Daniel felt the same way.

"I never thought I'd find this," Daniel murmured and pressed a kiss on his neck. He was spooning Corey from behind, and Corey was on the edges of sleep.

"What?" he asked, sleepily.

"Peace."

---

Corey took advantage of Sophie playing up in her room, her Barbies arranged around her in a big semi-circle. He asked Chloe and Amy to sit with him in their dad's office, and he closed the door.

"I have something to tell you, about Dad and Uncle Drake. Or show you. It's best you read it for yourselves."

He sat quietly as the girls huddled together over the paperwork. Chloe was quiet, Amy crying softly, and they held each other's hands as they turned the last page.

"He was this man? Uncle Drake?" Chloe finally asked.

She sounded as if she couldn't believe what she was reading, and Corey knew how she felt. He crouched in front of their chairs and rested his hands on their joined ones.

They talked far into the night, went from anger to hate to fury again.

But at the end of it, the three of them understood their father, had begun to come to terms with their uncle, and then they decided to keep the papers for Sophie, knowing that was a subject that would have to be dealt with in the future.

"How can Daniel even look at us?" Amy said, tears rolling down her face, "And the rest of them. How?"

"We're not our uncle, Amy. We never could be." He sighed and stood up, stretching out his cramped muscles. "Together," Corey said. "We'll tell Sophie when she's ready. We'll deal with it all as a family."

"We should hand this to the police, right?" Chloe asked, gripping the papers tight.

"Daniel, he wants to draw a line; he wants to live his life. Drake is dead, and we have to believe he didn't hurt anyone else. But with your permission, I want to ask the PI to research more, find out the extent of what he'd done, who else he may have hurt. Confidentially, until we know everything. What do you think?"

Chloe nodded, and Amy grasped his hand again, then pulled Chloe close.

"We'll work through this, together."

Corey thought that maybe then his family could also find peace.

## Epilogue

**Three years later**

SOMEHOW, DANIEL WAS IN CHARGE OF THE PUPPY VISIT.
How had that happened he didn't know, given he had zero
experience with organizing an event or making it a
success. The Legacy staff and guests had come into the
city to work with Steve's shelter and taken over a large
part of White Rock Lake Park that was now full of dogs.
At least thirty. From Bernie, the enormous shaggy St.
Bernard, to twins Elsa and Olaf, Cairn terriers that had
taken a liking to Corey's jeans.

The visit was a fundraising drive, but also raising
awareness of pets being suitable for all kinds of things. For
kids arriving at the shelter who'd lost everything, or those
who'd been brought there by the cops, all piss and vinegar,
and looking for someone to blame, or even the broken
ones the same as he'd been, who had no faith in the world.

Jack was there, in charge of nothing in particular,
standing to one side with a beer, right under the banner

which spelled out *puppy parade* in huge letters. He knew Riley was there somewhere. He'd brought Toby, the black lab, with him and was out there making friends with other dog owners. Flags had been pushed into flower pots, and all kinds of people were milling around, making donations, hugging and petting dogs, and generally having fun. There was food from a local catering company that specialized in barbecue, and people were eating, drinking, and laughing.

He'd pretty much achieved everything he'd set out to do.

"Good turnout," Jack said from right next to him, startling him.

"Jesus," he exclaimed.

"No, just Jack."

They exchanged smiles, comfortable in each other's company. "A couple of people wanted to talk to you about a possible adoption program connected to Legacy. Could be a good idea."

Enthusiasm gripped Daniel. The people passing through Legacy, the kids who stayed one night, or the ones who stayed longer, were getting to be more as the word spread. The entire ranch extended to have more living spaces, the garden bigger, with some produce being sold. Each young person who wanted it was offered a role on the ranch and a dog rescue of sorts would be perfect. Not just dogs. Maybe all kinds of animals.

"I'll talk to Kyle."

"Thought maybe you could take a run at it?"

That wasn't telling Daniel he would be doing it. This was suggesting that possibly it was time for Daniel to take on a project of his own. He'd made a life for himself at Legacy and, with Jack and Riley's blessing, had built a small place of his own a little away from the central ranch. It was only a two-bedroom, one bath, large kitchen, living space kind of thing, but it was his.

And Corey's.

And Sophie's.

They made quite the little family there.

They'd sold the Dryden house, invested the money. The PI turned up nothing else on Drake, but Corey had him looking into any leads that might ever come up. If there were other kids out there that someone in his family had wronged, then Corey said he wanted to do what he could. Amy was married to her Michael. Chloe was a permanent fixture at Steve's shelter, managing new intakes and placements. As for Corey, he was Daniel's partner, his lover, and currently halfway through writing his second novel. He also ran an education and skills program at Legacy, working with kids who, like Daniel, had missed school, helping them get their GED, getting some of them into college.

Everything was right in Daniel's world, and the idea of having something that would be uniquely *his* was exciting and scary.

"I'd love to do that, thank you."

Jack bumped elbows with him. "Don't thank me. It was Kyle's idea."

"Which is why he had me organize today?"

"Trial by fire." They grinned at each other. He didn't see Jack as a father figure, but as a friend, a good man who he could look up to and strive to make proud.

The nightmares barely happened now, and when they did, he had Corey there to hold him. Reliable, loving, gorgeous, sexy, Corey.

"Oh my god, you need to try this," Corey announced his arrival by thrusting a hot dog in a bun under Daniel's nose.

"Later," Jack drawled and walked over to where Riley was chatting to a group of enraptured people, all staring at him adoringly.

Daniel took the food and shook his head. "I still don't think serving hot dogs at a dog drive is a marketing success story."

Corey shoved him. "Eat the food, Danny."

"Kyle wants to set up a rescue place at Legacy, wants me to work it all out."

"That's awesome."

"We'd need it to be away from Legacy though. We don't want strangers running all over Legacy and loads of cars parked here."

"Right."

"And we'd need to think about permits. I should look into that." He pulled out his cell phone, a simple thing that Corey had demanded he carry with him. It wasn't an expensive one with bells and whistles, but it did have internet. He pressed to open it, but Corey snatched it from his hand.

"No looking now," he said. "Work can wait. Come with me."

He took Daniel's hand, and Daniel ate the hot dog as he was led away from the chaos to the shade of an oak tree. Amy and Michael were there, Chloe and her girlfriend holding hands, Sophie bouncing on her toes with excitement. Corey pulled him closer and then dropped his hand, moving to stand with his siblings.

"What is this," Daniel teased. "An intervention?" He laughed, and everyone was still smiling.

Then Corey looked focused. "I love you, Daniel."

"Okay." This sounded so damn serious, and the noise of the event around them faded away. "I love you too." He didn't have a problem admitting that in front of anyone. Life was too short to hold back on any kind of love.

"Daniel?" Corey reached into his pocket and pulled out something he couldn't see. Then he reached out, palm up, and there were two rings on there. The design was the same, one slightly larger. "Will you marry me?"

Daniel's heart stopped for a moment, fear, sadness, grief, pain, all slicing through him on instinct, and then abruptly, love filled all the broken parts, flooding him with a beauty he'd never seen. And he only had one answer.

"Yes."

Corey slipped one of the rings onto Daniel's finger. "It's a promise ring of sorts," he explained, then kissed Daniel's knuckles and handed him the other ring. "Until we decide when and where."

Daniel took the ring and Corey's hand. "When, as soon as possible. Where, Legacy."

Corey pulled him close, and they kissed, and he could hear clapping and whistling.

He didn't care about the noise. He kissed Corey thoroughly, and like that, Daniel's life changed direction again.

Straight ahead to a happy ever after.

**THE END**

## Next for the Campbell-Hayes of Texas

Read Connor Campbell-Hayes' story in the Christmas novella, Home for Christmas, coming November 2018.

## Have you read the Montana series?

If you liked the Texas and Legacy series'…

…then you will like my Montana series, with cowboys, a ranch, family, and love.

- Crooked Tree Ranch, Book 1
- The Rancher's Son, Book 2
- A Cowboy's Home, Book 3
- Snow in Montana, Book 4
- Second Chance Ranch, Book 5 - coming Summer 2018

---

## Crooked Tree Ranch, Montana, Book 1

**When a cowboy meets the guy from the city, he can't know how much things will change.**

On the spur of the moment, with his life collapsing around him, Jay Sullivan answers an ad for a business manager with an expertise in marketing, on a dude ranch in Montana.

With his sister, Ashley, niece, Kirsten and nephew, Josh, in tow, he moves lock stock and barrel from New York to Montana to start a new life on Crooked Tree Ranch.

Foreman and part owner of the ranch, ex rodeo star Nathaniel 'Nate' Todd has been running the dude ranch, for five years ever since his mentor Marcus Allen became ill.

His brothers convince him that he needs to get an expert in to help the business grow. He knows things have to change and but when the new guy turns up, with a troubled family in tow - he just isn't prepared for how much.

Have you read the Wyoming series?

---

Winter Cowboy (Book 1)

**Is it possible that love can be rekindled and become a forever to believe in?**

Micah Lennox left Whisper Ridge after promising the man he loved that he would never return. But as his sister begged for help when her life was in danger, the only way he knows to keep her and his nephew safe is to go home. Spending winter in Wyoming, when he'd promised never to return, opens too many old wounds, but he's on the run from justice which can't be far behind, and this is his last chance at redemption.

After a hostage situation leaves Doctor Daniel Sheridan struggling with PTSD, he returns to Whisper Ridge. Joining his dad in family practice is a balm to soothe his exhausted soul, and somehow, he finds a peace he can live with. That is until he meets Micah in a frozen graveyard, and the years of anger and feelings of betrayal boiling inside him, erupt.

Two broken men fight and scratch for their lives and that of their families, and somehow, in the middle of it all, they find each other.

## About the Author

RJ is the author of the over one hundred novels and discovered romance in books at a very young age. She realized that if there wasn't romance on the page, she could create it in her head, and is a lifelong writer.

She lives and works out of her home in the beautiful English countryside, spends her spare time reading and enjoying time with her family.

The last time she had a week's break from writing she didn't like it one little bit and she has yet to meet a bottle of wine she couldn't defeat.

www.rjscott.co.uk | rj@rjscott.co.uk

facebook.com/author.rjscott

twitter.com/Rjscott_author

instagram.com/rjscott_author

bookbub.com/authors/rj-scott

pinterest.com/rjscottauthor

Made in the USA
Lexington, KY
03 April 2019